Frenemiez II

Jock Phenix

I0553006

Publisher's Note: This is a work of fiction. Names, characters, places, and incidents are a product of the author's imagination. Locales and public names are sometimes used for atmospheric purposes. Any resemblance to actual people, living or dead, or to businesses, companies, events, institutions, or locales is completely coincidental.

Book Layout: Graphiz Designs
Cover Design: Graphiz Designs

Frenemiez II by Jock Phenix

Dedication

This book is dedicated to everyone that believed in me from the beginning and still do til this very day. In the beginning stages I remember straying from my writing because I was too busy with my Real Estate work but people would get on me asking when is Frenemiez coming out because I teased them from time to time with little snippets lol. That was inspiration whether they knew it or not.

It's nothing like seeing your creation become a reality and people actually enjoying your craft.I like to thank all my new readers from the bottom of my heart. You all inspired me to continue writing and were patient with me in the process. I love you all. I thank everyone that shared my posts on Facebook, retweeted my tweets on Twitter, and reposted my pics on Instagram.

I dedicate this book to you, my readers, my supporters, my fans. I hope that you enjoy Frenemiez PT 2 as well and continue to grow with me on my journey as an Author, I love yall.

In memory of my Aunt Carrie Bell Phenix and Linnei Hood, may you both rest in Heaven. Linnie I wish you could've witnessed all this, I know you would be proud.

Acknowledgements

I'm sitting here thinking about how blessed I am to be an pubished Author and on my second book. I'd like to that Brittani Willaims for believing in me and always givng it to me in the raw whenever I asked a question. I also have to give it up to my friends and family for believing in me. Johnny L Jones you know I have to give you recognition each and everytime. You continue to get me to think outside the box and to look at the bigger picture, couldn't ask for a better friend. Aries Phenix, my brother, I appreciate you listening to me whenever I had an idea and giving me great feedback to expand on those ideas. We spent many nights talking til 4AM, but I'm not trippin because it shows that we value our brotherhood. To my mother Gloria Phenix, I love you, I just want you to know I appreciate everything you've done for me. To my cousin kizzy Phoenix, I greatly appreciate you as well, whenever I needed you it was never a question or any hesitation.

Throwing my first book siging was pretty nerve wrecking and I'm not gone lie I was real nervous. But on some real shit I appreciate everyone that came to support me , Fella, Tony Reese, Carmel Ramsey I appreciate you, Debra Allen, Gil Nunley, Mia Shonte, Tasha Bias, Big Meech,Michelle Christine, Dan Terrill,Trish Stratus, Ryan Wroten, Chico, Tynecha Brown,Mike

Henderson, Kenyatta Craft,Al Cobb, Terrell Johnies, Tascha Harris, Bryson Willaims, JaNay Tobias, Bria Grant, Kam, and Heather Sowalla of WindyHill Editing,.

Can't forget all my Facebook, Twitter, and Instagram friends as well. Special shout out to Kwabena Nixon, Marc Brown and the Kiss Ultra Lounge establishment for making sure I was comfortable during my book signing. Can't forget Quiana Milton, Marv, Jawondee, Candace, Stephanie Findley, Law, Rashahn and KB for my t shirts, kim KPD, Disco Danny, Honor, Erica Mitchell, my homegirl Kendra, MaNisha, Tina Moffett, L.A,Shawn Allen got major love for you fam. My low end niggaz Mademan Meech, Scott, Lou, Slick, Sir, thanks for your support.

Drae Howell, B Shake, Lamar Hall, D Wright, Slick, Will Cocroft,Tiffany Rumley,Riles & Dee Riley, Esha Shari, Tyrice hardin, Devon Ramsey, The Ghani's, Tamairo Moutry, Selina Johnson, DeAngelo Ritchie, Princess Camidee, Curt Kleeba,Shamon Johnson, Ronnie wells,Nancy Pitman, Shannon Jefferson, Tonia Stewart, Quiana Jasper, Melinda Currie, Sonja Jackson, Bobby Jones, Robert Bellamy, Joy, Moffie, Jizzles Sandwich shop, Ms Ceree, Tomeka Ford Studio 089, Letoya Killebrew,Roosevelt smith, Brontay Butts, Briana Nicole, Nakeeta Shackelford, Kita Aisha, HK, Myrical, Latrice Jinor, and Red Carson,

I can never forget about my Phenix/Phoenix family from MKE, to Lousianna, and across the map, we all may not get along but we all family. To my Lil Cousin Devontae hold yo head in there, stay strong, and bounce back and do better this time. Yvette Jones til this day you still remain a loyal friend to me and I appreciate that from the bottom of my heart. To my lil sis Nesie Woodley, stay you, that's all I'm gonna say, love. Can't forget about my bro James aka Nas Owens, Big Duece, Quiana and Cicely Thomas , Nicole and Resco,Trina Porter, Tone Fitzgerald, KG, Trae Day, Dino, Chris Coffee, Ronnie, Rico, Tuco, Turtle, and the rest of my folks on the Eastside on all sides, Latronda Mitchell, Ola,Tiffany Pitts, Megayn Bera, J Marie thanks for putting my book cover on your J Marie magazine too, I appreciated that blessing.

Gotta give it up to my hometown Lake Providence, Louisianna. R.I.H Carrie Bell Phenix, Linnie Hood, Lil Lonnie, Archie Brown, Alexis Patterson, Big Earl, Phonzo, and Dontre Hamilton.

If I forgot to mention your name just know that it wasn't intentional and I will bless you in my next book.

Chapter 1

Two months passed since Rudy's brutal murder. Boss and Trouble were tired of sitting still, they were ready to start hustling, but they just had to wait on the green light from Truth. Two weeks passed since Boss had any dope, and Truth knew he had to get back on his grind before his squad went broke. Truth had a clever network set up to dump the bricks. He was going to put his head lieutenant, Boss, in charge of streets distributions, while Trouble ran the trap house they had on the Eastside.

Truth decided on playing the back while Boss got his shine on so he could focus on ways to launder his money. After hearing about all the recent indictments, Truth wanted to become a myth in the streets so nothing would be traced back to him.

"What's your plan for today, baby?" Jazzie asked.

"I think I'm 'bout to put these bricks on the streets, I been laying low long enough," Truth replied.

"You have been chilling, baby. Well, me and Raquel gone run to the nail shop then take her kids to Chuck E. Cheese, so I'ma be busy all day, okay?" Jazzie stated as she kissed Truth on the cheek.

"Don't be up in Chuck E. Cheese getting drunk, y'all know the kids supposed to be the ones having fun not ya'll grown butt's," Truth joked.

"Whatever Truth, all they sell is cheap shit in there, I drink top shelf," She bragged.

"Shut up, you need any money?" Truth asked as he stuck his hand inside his pocket.

"You know I do," Jazzie replied.

He peeled off a few C-Notes then handed them to Jazzie.

"Get the Vet washed too, damn that mudda fucka dirty," He expressed.

"I will damnnn, the car wash be too packed," Jazzie whined.

"Well, get yo ass up early and be the first one thurr," He ordered.

"You know I don't get up early, Truth." She whined.

"When the King Cobra be on brick yo' ass do."

They both burst out laughing as they got dressed. Truth didn't care where Jazzie was going, getting his bricks off was his only concern.

Truth decided it was time to give his squad a call and let them know it was time to feed the streets. He called Boss first. Boss was chilling in his basement, playing Mortal Kombat on his Playstation1 when his phone started vibrating on his lap.

"Who dis?"

"Me nigga," Truth shot back.

"What up East?"

"Whuz zatnin East, I'm gone holla at the plug today, so be ready when I call, okay Folks?"

Boss sat the Playstation controller down quickly, "I'm ready now East. Man, itz 'bout time."

"Oh, I got a surprise fo' you too, bruh, I hope you can handle it," Truth grinned while rubbing his chin.

"What? You know I hate surprises," Boss stated as he gazed up at the ceiling.

"Simmer down Folks, you'll see in a second, just be ready when I call."

Truth ended the call then called Trouble.

"Whoadaaay, whuzz zatnin!!" Truth yelled.

"Whuzz shakin' shagaay!" Trouble replied.

"Mane itz time to eat. I'm 'bout to put yo' ass on fo' real; I bet you thought I was jackin' too, huh bruh?"

"Huh bruh, what I gotta do?" Trouble inquired eagerly.

"Be at the spot on Palmer and Chambers in a hour. Boss gone drop a package off to ya, and put you up on how the spot is ran," Truth explained.

"Huh bruh, okay okay, letz do this shit."

Trouble was ready to make some money.

"Cuz, if you follow what I'm 'bout to say to you, you'll be a rich mudda fucka in no time." Trouble was eager to hear what Truth had to say so he was all ears. "One, never let nann nigga know how much money you got stashed, money brings jealousy, cuz. Two, never let a mudda fucka know yo next move, real gangstaz move in silence, bruh. Three, never trust nobody, I mean nobody, a nigga will set yo ass up quick! Four, don't get high off yo' own supply, regardless of what you saw Scarface do in the movie, you'll fuck around and be yo' best customer. Five, never bust a move where you lay you head at. I know thatz self explanatory, cuz. Six, watch who you give credit to, we in the biz to make money not loose money, you can't trust a crackhead as far as you can see them. Seven, keep the fam and yo' biz separate, that shit don't mix, two different worlds cuz. Eight, never keep no weight on you, keep a flunky around to hold that shit. Nine, stay the fuck out the way of police, try not to bring too much attention to ya self. Ten, don't front a nigga shit if he don't have the clientele to move that shit, and last, I get paid first before you pocket yours." Truth instructed.

Damn, this nigga on his shit, Trouble thought as he listened to his big cuz lecture.

"And stack yo' paper cuz I'm frontin' you 'til the money start flowing so before you know it you should be able to cop a brick on yo' own," Truth explained. "Don't even trip cuz I gotcha," Trouble assured while grinning. "Once I see a mill or two, I'm done cuz. This shit ain't a career, it's a steppin' stone to something bigger and better. I got a hungry lawyer on deck ready to eat up any case,

so if you get knocked keep yo' mouth shut, and I'll post yo' bail."
Truth explained.

Trouble hung on every word like a soldier taking orders from his drill sergeant. He was astonished at the wealth of street knowledge Truth had. He never knew he was 'bout his business like that.

"Cuz, I gotcha. What was that, the hustlaz commandments? I feel like I'm 'bout to go to war or sumthin'," Trouble joked.

Truth bit down on his lip and shook his head.

"This is war, bruh, ain't no turning back, so please don't take this shit as a joke," Truth snapped.

"Damn cuz, my fault, simmer down," Trouble countered.

"Cuz, shitz real out chea, I need you on top of yo' game at all times," He stressed.

"Say no more, cuz."

"Well, meet me at the trap in a few hours." The men said their good byes and hung up.

Truth made sure his squad kept burnout cell phones. He didn't believe in hustling with phones that were turned on through a phone company because the calls were traceable. Every other month he switched phones for extra precautions. In the game if your conscience told you to do something and you ignored it, that was usually your demise.

Truth loved the way his '95 Impala handled on the highway. As he headed towards the South Side down I-94, he punched the gas accelerating up to 80 mph, then broke the speed back down to the speed limit. Truth exited on National Avenue then called his home girl, Mileena. Mileena was his girlfriend back in High School.

Their relationship only lasted for a month, because her mother didn't approve of her daughter dating outside their race. They stayed in contact over the years, and later became business associates, as well as fuck buddies.

Mileena stood 5'2", was very curvaceous, had jet black curly shoulder length hair, full lips, and pretty golden skin with a hints of freckles sprinkled throughout her face. She was one hundred percent Dominican and gangster as fuck. Mileena was an excellent chef in the kitchen when it came to cooking dope. Whenever the South Side was suffering from a lil drought, she would bring the business to Truth, who brought the money to his plug, Rudy.

What Mileena didn't know was Truth was the brickman now and held the key to the city. They say nine tenths of the law is possession, but in reality it's positioning, and Mileena was in the perfect position unknowingly.

****

"Whuz zatnin hot gurl?" Truth greeted as he rubbed the stubbles on his chin.

"Shit, just over here on 14th N National chillin' with my home girls. Why, whatz up, Papi?" Mileena stated in her strong Spanish accent.

"I need you in the kitchen, I'm hungry," Truth replied, speaking in code.

Mileena knew exactly what Truth was referring to so she stood up and walked a few feet away from her friends.

"What's in it for me, King Ding A Ling?" Mileena responded. Truth couldn't help but smile. "You know I'll do anything fo' yo crazy black ass," Mileena made known as she ran her fingers through her hair.

"Well, meet me at the honey comb hideout in fifteen minutes. I just got off the highway," he instructed.

"I'll be there in a sec, let me wrap shit up with my home girls then I'm on my way." She responded.

"Who was that, Mileena?" Sasha inquired.

"Damn bitch, you nosey. Anyway I gotta go, I'll get up with you bitches in a sec. Okay?" She said as she grabbed her purse, and continued to her car.

"Ok bitch, we'll be at Peto's house, so come by there. He got some Cali bud on deck," Sasha yelled out.

"Peto got some fuckin' Cali! He bogus! He didn't tell me shit! I'm gonna cuss his ass out for holding out on a bitch!" Mileena stopped to state.

"I'll let him know you pissed at him, Mileena," Sasha laughed.

"Yeah tell his ass, now let me get out of here. I'll catch up to y'all in a few."

She was in a rush to see Truth.

As Truth drove down National Avenue, he tripped off how the Southside was so different from the Northside. The Hispanics ran the Southside, and everybody knew it. They repped their culture and gangs with the utmost pride. Their flags could be seen everywhere. The Hispanics drove the hottest low-riders, and gang-banged way harder than the Northside.

Truth was familiar with the Hispanic culture growing up on the Eastside of Milwaukee. He loved when his Hispanic homies' moms cooked. He had a thing for Hispanic foods.

Truth was thirsty so he made a stop at the gas station on 27th and National. He hopped out of the car with his hat cocked to the right, which was a no no in certain parts of the Southside. Truth headed inside the gas station not paying attention to his surroundings, which was a violation of the G-Code. Once he found his preferred drink, a 32oz. Gatorade, he headed towards the counter.

While Truth waited in line, two Latino goons walked through the door dressed in yellow Nike T-shirts, yellow and black Dukey's, black Dickies pants that sagged off their ass, and Pittsburg Pirate hats banged to the left. One of the goons bumped Truth purposely and kept it moving.

"S'cuse you bruh!" Truth muttered aggressively.

The young goon ice grilled Truth as he stared him up and down, you could tell he was geeked from the white powder that still lined his nostrils.

"My fault Lord," the goon shot back, disrespecting Truth to the fullest.

Truth frowned back at the goon.

"Nigga, you see how I'm bangin' my hat, respect my G!" Truth snarled at the thug.

"Fuck yo' nation nigga, itz King Nation or nothing, bro!" The young gangster claimed as he swayed his head from side to side mean mugging Truth.

Mileena's gas hand was on "E" so she stopped at the nearest gas station.

"Hmm, what's da odds of me and Truth stopping at the same gas station?" Mileena pondered as she slapped her car into park.

Mileena reach under her seat and retrieved a baby 380 Kel-Tec semi auto. She didn't put nothing past anybody and didn't want to get caught slipping under any circumstances.

Truth threw up his forks while he mean mugged the two goons back.

"Gangstaz make the world go round, lil bitches," he stated brashly.

Pissed by Truth's bold response on their side of town, one of the goons drew his 45 blue stainless steel Taurus and pointed it at Truth's face. The customers that were in line stormed out of the gas station. The cashier was trembling so hard she nearly fainted.

"You better kill me, nigga, cuz if you don't thatz yo' azz mane," Truth delivered cold heartedly.

It was a stare down between the men, death was in the air. The goons were waiting on Truth to just flinch the wrong way. Mileena entered the gas station still bobbing her head to the music she was bumping in her car. When she saw the look on the cashier face she immediately got on point.

"Jose, what da fuck you doing! Put that shit up before I take it and pop yo' ass!" Mileena instructed seriously.

"You know this black fucker or something!" Jose asked with a look of confusion.

"Yes, thatz my nigga, fool! This the nigga I been telling you 'bout, he's Truth."

Jose's chest fizzled down like a balloon.

"Ahh damn my nig, my fault homie, I didn't know who you were," Jose apologized with a slight grin.

"No prob bruh, thanks Mileena," Truth stated while cutting his eye at Jose.

"I'm sorry 'bout this Truth, thatz my lil cuzzin. You gotta excuse him, he a lil crazy," Mileena confessed as she rolled her eyes at Jose.

Truth cracked his knuckles then nodded his head.

"Yo' cuz almost got his head knocked off his shoulders, you know I keep my banger on me," Truth barked.

"Chill out Papi, go pump my gas while I go grab some chips and a Pepsi," Mileena commanded, separating him from her cousin.

"Only fo' you, Mami," Truth grumbled as he shook his head.

"Shut up with yo fine ass," Mileena flirted. "Don't ever pull no shit like that again, Jose! You could've got killed in here!" She yelled.

"Mileena, we're sorry. We didn't know who the fuck dude was," Jose pouted.

"I gotta go," Mileena hissed while shaking her head at her cousins.

Mileena trailed Truth back to the stash house. Once inside, Truth went straight to the refrigerator, grabbed two Coronas and handed one to Mileena. She popped the top off on the counter top then downed the beer like it was water.

"So how much we cooking?" Mileena asked as she slammed the empty bottle on the counter.

"Don't know yet, let me holla at Boss and see something real quick."

Truth gave Boss a call on his burn out cell.

"Who dis?" Boss stated calmly.

"Me fool! How many yickens you think you can handle?" Truth inquired.

Boss didn't know what to say, he knew things had to be looking good on Truth's end.

"Umm two," Boss replied.

"That mean four," Truth shot back.

"Whoah East, I don't think you heard me," Boss countered quickly.

"I don't think you heard me, nigga," Truth replied then hung up.

"I'm giving Boss four bricks, so I'ma need at least five bricks whipped," Truth confirmed as he scratched his head.

"Okay, but I gotta get some dick first," Mileena stressed as she bit her bottom lip.

"I should've known you was up to something, gurl."

He loved when she was so upfront about whatever she wanted..

"And I bought some condoms while we were at the gas station so ain't no excuses, Papi." Mileena teased. Truth loved how strong willed Mileena was, in fact, it turned him on. Mileena walked up to Truth, looked him in his eyes, stuck her hand inside his pants then started fondling his penis. "I see he hard, let me get a quickie, nicca," Mileena purred as she gripped the shaft of Truth's snake.

Truth dropped his pants and boxers quickly. Mileena slid the condom onto Truth's full manhood, then turned around so he could mount her doggy style.

Truth spit on his middle finger to lubricate Mileena's juicebox then slid right in, giving her every inch of his shaft. As Truth delved deeper into her sweet honey pot, she moaned out in ecstasy.

"Ohhh Papi! Pull my hair! Harder! Harder!"

Truth followed her commands, punishing her from the back.

"You like that, huh mami! You like dat shit!" Truth chanted as sweat dripped down his forehead.

"Come on give me that nut! Give me that nut!" Mileena yelled and started slamming her ass back against Truth's pelvic area as he stood on his tippy toes gripping her ass. Mileena's body clinched up as she started to reach her climax. "Ahh! Shiittt! I'm cumin' Papi!"

Mileena's body jerked uncontrollably as her juices flowed down her leg. Truth couldn't hold it in anymore. He exploded inside the condom then flopped on top of Mileena panting hard.

Truth slid the condom off, walked into his bathroom then ran some water inside the condom to see if it had any leaks. Satisfied with the results, he flushed the used condom down the toilet.

Mileena and Truth took a quick shower to wash away the stench of sex then got back to the task at hand, turning powder into crack.

Truth went down to the basement, pulled the lever that opened the fake wall then stared at the pile of white bricks. He smiled as dollars signs glittered in his eyes.

"I'm rich bitch!" He yelled as he grabbed four bricks.

Truth's plan was to turn three bricks into five and give Boss a clean one. He grabbedtwo three- inch deep Pyrex pots and a triple beam from the stash then headed back upstairs. Once back upstairs, Truth made sure all the curtains were shut and the doors were secured then handed Mileena a face mask and some latex gloves.

"Grab all the baking soda out the fridge, Mami," he instructed.

"Okay Doc," Mileena stated with a chuckle.

"Chill with dat Doc shit," Truth stated sternly.

"Damn, I was just fuckin' with cha," she replied.

"Well, this ain't the time fo' games. We got enough dope here to bury us under the Federal Pen," Truth reminded her.

"Ol' super sensitive ass nigga," Mileena mumbled under her breath.

She stared at the scorpion stamps on the bricks in front of her then began cutting them open. Cocaine dust filled the air. This would've been a cocaine snorter's dream just to inhale the dust alone. Once the brick was dumped into the Pyrex pot, they poured just enough water in each pot to break the powder down.

They placed the pots on the stove under medium heat, cooking the cocaine down to an oil base. Next, they dumped enough baking soda into the Pyrex, turned on their blenders and beat the mixture together 'til it was an even color. Lastly, they stuck a knife in the middle of the pot then placed it in the freezer to cool and harden the dope.

Truth waited about fifteen minutes before he checked the Pyrex's to see if the substance was solid, luckily it was. They wiggled the knives to get the dope to loosen up, pulled it out of the

Pyrex then dumped the dope on top of some newspaper. Truth tapped on his finished product to see how hard it was, Mileena followed suit.

Next, they took a lighter and ran the flames over the bricks of cocaine to see if it turned black in any spots, luckily it didn't. They did that to make sure the baking soda was evenly spread throughout the bricks, also so that the crack heads wouldn't complain about their pipes turning black. Truth placed one brick on the triple bean to get the exact weight of the cook up. It came out to be 1,505 grams. Mileena weighed up the bricks she cooked; one came back to be 1,570 grams the other 1,565 grams.

"I see you out did me again, Mami," Truth grinned.

"Itz all in the wrist, Papi, itz all in the wrist," Mileena bragged as she moved her wrist in a circular motion.

"Take 130 grams out fo' yo' self, boo."

Truth always rewarded Mileena well for helping him in the kitchen.

"Thanks Papi, if anybody calls for some of this butta I'll send them yo' way," Mileena stated happily.

"Good lookin out mami, I sure need all the help I can get," he replied with a smile.

Truth called Boss up and told him to come see him. Boss stopped everything he was doing then rushed off to the Southside. Twenty minutes later the doorbell rang, startling Truth and Mileena.

"Truth, you expecting anyone?" Mileena asked with her eyes bucked.

"Yeah my boy, Boss, let me go check the security camera to make sure itz him though."

Truth kept a chopper by the back door, so he was prepared for any jacker to trying to pull a move. Truth was relieved when he saw that it was his head lieutenant, Boss at the door. The doorbell rang again, and Mileena stood up to go grab the chopper. She wasn't taking nothing lightly.

"Relax ma, itz my nigga, Boss," Truth assured her.

"Shit, I was scared, it is too much dope up in here." She was relieved.

"I was scared too, but we all good now." Truth unlocked the bolts on the steel door, then greeted Boss with a hug. "My fault for taking so long to answer the door, bruh. A nigga can't be too safe ya dig?" Truth apologized.

"No prob Folks, I totally feel ya. Hey Mileena, you over there looking like Eva Mendez and shit," Boss stated.

Mileena waved at Boss, "Heeey Boss, I see you put on a few pounds," she joked.

"That's good living, baby; steak and shrimp," He boasted.

"Shit, I need to eat what you been eating then," Mileena flirted back as she punched Boss on his arm.

"Where is da P? I need some shit thatz baking soda free!" Boss rapped as he took a seat on the couch.

Boss never learned the whip game; he figured he didn't have time to be slaving over a hot stove when he could count on Truth to do it. Truth actually paid a cat out of Chicago ten G's to teach him the whip game. Truth stepped in the kitchen.

"So what's the ticket on this shit?" Boss yelled from the couch.

"For straight raw itz twenty-seven G's for you, and cooked twenty- fo'.""

Truth's eyebrows rose up a lil. He was waiting for a reaction from Boss. Boss thought for a second then did some quick math.

"That ain't bad; I can work with them numbers. I can dump the cooked shit off for thirty G's the way shit is out here."

Boss could smell the money already.

"Well, I'm giving you three hard and one soft," explained Truth.

"Cool, I got one of them sold already too," Boss threw in.

"Oh I almost forgot, take Trouble a split and have him ball up three zips (oz's) and dime the rest up. He got the spot on P-C now, and you running all the weight. So whatever you need, just holla, we on fo real now," Truth instructed.

"On what! I thought you was jackin' about that shit, fool." Boss uttered.

"I know you did, nigga. Make sho' yo' ass drive back safe too, bruh," Truth stated in a concerned voice.

"You ain't gotta stress it, I ain't tryna get popped with all this shit. On my momma, I'm 'bout to fuck these boyz up thinking they got the streets on lock!"

Truth shook his head then grinned.

"Boss, don't start blowing money like yo' azz crazy either. Remember what happened to J-Dub, make sure you stack yo' shit up, bruh, fo' real. A nigga gotta be prepared for the worst case scenario." Truth tried to educate his partner.

"Be easy Truth, let me fuck dis cow, I got this folks," Boss laughed as he gave Truth some dap.

Boss never had this much dope in his possession at one time, he was ready to be "The Man" now, something he always dreamed about.

Chapter 2

"Whuzz zatnin, King Mitch?" Truth greeted.

"Hey Truth, you here to pick up your jewelry?" Mitch questioned.

"Yup, how much I owe you, bruh?"

King Mitch started punching numbers on his calculator like an accountant, then showed Truth the total.

"You see what that say, but I'ma plug ya, give me thirty thousand, and we can call it even." Truth thought about contesting the price, but deep inside he knew King Mitch was giving him a play. "Ya'll need some new chains to go with these pieces?" King Mitch asked.

Truth rubbed his chin as he pondered for a second.

"I do need a new chain since I got a new piece, what you got for me, Bruh?" Truth stated after much contemplation.

"Well, I got a thirty inch Rolex necklace, itz hot too. Niggaz sleeping on these Rolex necklaces too. I can give it to you for $3,500, and for your girl I got a 14k or Platinum eighteen inch Rolex chain for $2,500."

King Mitch handed Truth the necklaces while smiling ear to ear. Truth inspected the necklace then gave King Magic a head nod.

"I'll take both necklaces in Platinum, what you think baby?"

Jazzie shrugged her shoulders as her face glowed.

"I like them. I think you should get them." She concluded.

"Magic, since I'm buying a Rolex necklace, I'ma need a Platinum Presidential Rolex watch to match the chain and a Platinum pinky ring. Matter fact, give me that one right thurr," Truth stated as he pointed at the Platinum Princess cut invisible set 3.5 Diamond ring.

King Mitch continued to punch numbers into his calculator. Once he was done tallying up the total, he looked up at Truth.

"Okay now, that will be $75,000 with my discount," he explained.

"How we gone do this?" Truth asked.

"Let me worry 'bout the paper work. I'll call you once the store closed to do the money transaction, cool?"

"No prob King Mitch."

Both men shook hands. Truth was definitely satisfied with King Mitch's craftsmanship.

****

Business was going good for Truth. He was making money hand over fist. Boss was making a name for himself while Trouble was holding down his trap house. Everybody was eating while Truth played the background like a true Capo. He made sure his crew stacked their money up for a rainy day. Truth kept a retainer with his lawyer. He knew each day was a gamble, so he wanted to be prepared for the worst.

Truth turned thirty bricks into fifty, and made $720,000 dollars. He was down to twenty bricks and knew if he wanted to continue his operation he would need a new plug, but who? He didn't want a Milwaukee plug because he would be paying too much per brick. Plus he didn't want anybody knowing how much dope he was copping.

Truth learned from the OG's before him that the best way to wash your dirty money is through a few front businesses, which was next on his agenda. After having a business meeting with his lawyer, Truth was advised to open some front businesses like a car wash, a candy store, and a salon for starters. The first business he opened up was a smoke shop on the Eastside. He sold drug paraphernalia, nachos, junk food, C.D's and bootleg videos.

Truth wanted to open a salon but needed to find a vacant building. He snapped his finger and thought, Heaven is a Realtor. That can be my excuse for getting at her. Jazzie know plenty of hoes, so I know she can find somebody with a cosmetology license to put in the shop. Truth had it all figured out. He pulled Heaven's business card out of his wallet then set up a meeting with her for the following week. They met at Perkin's Soul Food Restaurant.

Truth had a taste for some greens, hot water cornbread, macaroni, and smothered pork chops. Heaven wasn't that hungry so she ordered a slice of caramel cake and a cup of coffee.

"So you looking to invest in some property?" Heaven inquired as she took a sip of her black coffee.

Truth didn't respond right away, he was too busy stuffing his face.

"S'cuse me Heaven, I'm hungry as hell," Truth mumbled with a mouth full of food, Heaven turned her head and smiled.

"Damn, wipe yo' mouth," She stated with her face scrunched up.

"My fault Ma, a nigga hungry as fuck," Truth stated as he wiped his mouth off then smiled at Heaven. "Okay, now I need some space to open a salon/ barbershop," he explained.

"You have a preferable location, and how many square feet you gone need?" She questioned while taking notes.

"I'm thinking in a high traffic area, maybe on Capitol, Burleigh, North Ave., or Center St. I at least want it to be big enough to accommodate eight chairs, six sinks, maybe a play area for the kids, a few vending machines, and a booth to sell hair products."

Heaven took note of all the details on her notepad.

"Sounds like a good idea. Have you thought about adding a small spa? That would be different from what all the other shops are doing, and that space you talking about using as a play area could be used to make more money, if you eliminated that idea."

Truth rubbed his chin then smurked, "Thanks for putting me up on game, Heaven. I think I'll do it like that," he insisted.

"Plus, I know a group of students about to graduate from MATC next month. I could refer them to you once you get your shop up and running," she added.

"I'd appreciate that. So what you got for me?" Truth asked as he finished

up his last bite.

"I have a building on Fond Du Lac and Burleigh that was a furniture store, one on 38th N. Burleigh, one on MLK and Lloyd, one on 55th N. North, and one on Appleton, between Capitol & 76th, one on. "

Truth cut Heaven off in the middle of her sentence. He was satisfied with the locations she mentioned.

"Which building has the most space?" Truth asked.

"Well, I have the building on Fond Du Lac and Burleigh, like I said that used to be a furniture store. It's very spacious. You may even have some space left over too," she explained.

"When can I view it?" He asked.

"I got the keys now, we can run over there now if you got time," she said as grabbed the keys from her purse.

"You ain't said shit, letz roll."

He was ready to put all his plans in motion.

Truth pulled out a knot and laid a fifty dollar bill on the table.

"I'll be right back with your change," the waitress stated.

"Nah, keep it, and tell Andel she put her foot in dem greens," he praised.

"I will and thanks for the tip," she continued cleaning the table.

"No prob, you made me feel like I was at home so I gotta return the love," Truth interjected.

"Bless yo' heart son, girl, you got a real man on yo' side," the waitress complimented.

Heaven grinned, "He's not my man. He's a client of mine," she corrected.

"Oh, ok," the waitress replied as she winked at Truth.

****

When they arrived at the vacant building Truth envisioned the salon being in business. Where would my customers park? Truth thought.

"For a building this size, where would my clients park, Heaven?" He asked.

"That's a good question; maybe you need something at a strip mall." She replied, while thumbing through the listings. "BINGO! I got some space at the Silvermill Mall that would be perfect. Plus, security patrols the area, and you'd draw in clients that were already shopping at the surrounding stores," she explained.

"Well, letz go over thurr so I can look at this building," Truth stated excitedly.

Fifteen minutes later they were at the Silvermill Mall. Heaven explained what repairs needed to be done to get the salon up to code and running. They flirted back and forth as she took Truth on a tour of the building. He was amazed at Heaven's professionalism; in fact, it turned him on.

"When can I take you to dinner?" Truth inquired, jumping off the subject.

Heaven blushed. She wanted to take care of business before pleasure and wasn't about to let Truth charm her.

"We just had lunch, Truth. Let's keep this professional. I already told you I'm not playing second to no one, so when you ready for a real woman, you got my number. Now back to this building, do you need financing?"

Truth tried to save face after being rejected so he mustered up a smile as he responded,

"Nah, just put an offer in to the bank. If they accept, give me a call, and I'll have my lawyer handle errthang."

Truth had some business to tend to so he ended the meeting. They both shook hands then parted ways.

A young black man that's about his business, I like that. He just need to get rid of Jazzie gold digging ass, Heaven thought. She hopped in her SUV heading back to her office thinking, He'll come around sooner or later. The smell of his cologne lingered around her as she closed her eyes to remember their meeting.

****

"Hey Trouble," Sparkle flirted as she sashayed past the trap house, trying to catch his attention.

"Whuzz zatnin Shawty? When you gone let a gangsta tap dat?" Trouble blurted as he grabbed his crotch.

"All you gotta do is act like it, nigga," Sparkle shot back as she rested her hand on her wide hips.

"I'ma get at yo' ass tonite then, Ma. Money over errthang first, you know my motto," He informed the girl.

"We'll see, you know how to find me, nicca."

As Sparkle strutted off with her son, Trouble thought, I'ma act a donkey on dat azz. Trouble was slowly becoming a hood legend on the Eastside. He was bangin' all the hood rats in the hood. Word was spreading fast on how he was punishing the pussy. Trouble went back inside the spot. The weeks intake needed to be counted before Truth made his rounds. He was doing good now, he went from a split to a brick.

Trouble would pay for half the brick while Truth fronted him the other half. He learned the whip game so that helped him stack up a lot of money. Trouble sold nothing but 20's and 8 balls out of his trap house, and it stayed booming. He was definitely eating good now, it was no comparison to how he was living in Louisiana. He took Truth's advice, "stack first so you can spend later."

When they went out Truth paid for everything, even if they had their own money. That was his way of showing appreciation for his squad. Boss was doing numbers too. He went from copping three bricks to five in no time. Truth wanted his team to stack their money because he hadn't planned on being in the game for the long haul. He was sitting on 1.3 million, had a few investments in the works and was thinking about getting into Real Estate and flipping houses. Truth vowed not to get popped off like the hustlers before him. He was going to learn from the old heads mistakes.

****

Jazzie's conscious started eating at her. She felt bad for leaving Law while he was fresh on his bid. Jazzie made a visit to Law's mother to catch one of his calls from jail. She even started writing him frequently and sending him money that Truth gave her.

Jazzie needed to smoke so she went into her stash and rolled a blunt. She was stressed and needed to get some shit off her chest. After the blunt was blazed, Jazzie savored the aroma of the weed smoke. She wished she was somewhere on Mars without a care in the world. She grabbed a pen and pad, gazed at the ceiling and began to write.

Dear Law,

I hope this letter reaches you in the best of health. I've been thinking about all the good times we shared and I almost cried. You were my provider, my lover, my best friend, and my father figure. I know that sounds crazy. My father was never there for me, but you taught me so much about life, and how to survive.

When you left I was so scared and confused. I never planned on being with Truth this long, but I figured since he was so young I'd milk him like the way you taught me to break a trick. Here's 2G's, I know I'm out of pocket and owe you more, but I hope you can forgive me. This pussy will always be yours and my mind too. I pray you come home soon so we can rekindle our relationship.

Your bottom bitch,
Jazzie

Jazzie sprayed a few drops of perfume on the letter then sealed it.

"I hope this smooth things out between me and Law. I really do miss him," Jazzie whispered as she wiped a tear from her eye.

She dropped the letter in the mailbox then headed over to Raquel's house so they could go to Northridge Mall.

****

"Mail for Mr. Riley," said the fat pale skinned prison guard. Law walked up to the officer station and grabbed his mail. Before he could take a look at the envelope, the C.O. handed him another piece of mail. "Oh, you have a money receipt too."

Law smiled, he had not been expecting a money receipt. Law's heart skipped a beat when he saw who had wrote and sent the money receipt.

"This bitch still got love fo' a pimp," Law mumbled as he glanced at the money receipt. "Bitch betta have my money, she lucky I don't put a hit out on her ass."

Law wanted to reach out and touch Jazzie, but he knew he would be up for appeal soon so he kept his cool. So far Law stacked up five G's since Jazzie had been hitting his hand. He had all the property an inmate could have, two pair of Gucci Loafers, two pair of Air Jordan's, one pair of Dukeys, five pair of designers jeans, five dress shirts, T.V, radio, typewriter, clippers, two jogging suits, two pairs of Versace sunglasses, a mass amount of commissary, and a burn out cell phone.

Law wanted his prison stay to be as comfortable as possible so it didn't seem like he was doing hard time.

"What we cooking tonight, Law?" His celly asked as he rubbed his empty stomach.

"Shiddddd, we might as well hook up some nachos, see if you can get somebody to bring some chicken breast from the kitchen."

"Chicken breast? Damn nigga, you tryna clown tonight," Law's celly replied.

"I gotta treat myself whether I'm in jail or not, ya dig?" Law explained to his fellow cellmate.

"I feel ya, pimpin," his celly agreed as he grabbed his room key and left the room.

Chapter 3

Boss got word that it was sweet in Appleton, WI. 8balls were going for $250, which was almost three times the amount they went for in Milwaukee. Once he figured out a way to stick and move, his plan was to hit the small town real hard and then disappear. Appleton was a predominately white town, with the exception of the black people that migrated from Chicago.

Asians were also making their way into the small town, kicking up dust. Appleton wasn't used to the gang banging culture up close and personal. The closet they ever saw any gang activity was in a rap video or a movie.

Boss and Truth were in a heated battle, playing Mortal Kombat on Playstation. Boss' basement was plushed out, he remodeled it into a rec room equipped with a Viper Reno Billiards Pool Table, a

Gold's Gym weight set, and three T.V's with game systems hooked up to them.

"Truth, I got some niggaz that be hustling up in Appleton. They tryna fuck with me," Boss stated as he rapidly tapped on his joystick buttons.

"How you hook up with them niggaz?" Truth asked as he laid his controller down.

"I was up there hoopin' with my cousin boyfriend, right. We went out that night and run into some niggaz up there hustlin', Fam. I chopz it up with dem, and they told me how them white folks going crazy for dis white shit," Boss replied.

"On whuut? Do we need to send some niggaz from the hood out thurr?" Truth asked.

"Nah. peep this, zips goin' for $1600 easy up there! I can step on a brick, and let my cousin boyfriend get that shit off," Boss snapped mischievously.

"You don't need me then, bruh, that can be yo' own lil thang," Truth stated.

"I was just running it by you to get yo' opinion on thangz," Boss emphasized as he stared at Truth waiting on a response.

"Shiiiddd, expansion is always good, bruh, as long as you do yo' homework first," Truth insisted.

"Thanks for yo' input fam. The more dope I run through, the richer we all getting." Boss replied as he gave Truth some dap.

"Thatz what I wanna see, errbody comin' up. I don't want to be the only one holding major chips between us. What if I need a loan? I wanna be able to come to one of y'all," Truth made known as he beat Boss for the sixth time.

"I'm running low anyways, bruh, so get with me asap," Truth stated.

"Okay Folks. When you gone step yo' car game up, nigga? You got way too much money to be rolling in that SS," Boss joked.

"I ain't in no rush to go to jail. I can cop foreign now if I wanted to. I'm tryna build my empire and get a paper trail behind me before I start flossing like that," Truth stressed sternly.

"You remember what dat nigga Scarface said? First you get the money, then you get the power," He recited.

"I hear ya nigga, but no matter what you say, you still need to step yo' whip game up," Boss countered with a slight chuckle.

They continued to play Mortal Kombat while sipping on Hennessy 'til their fingers were sore.

****

Truth sank his body into the butter soft Italian leather couch as his mind wandered. ESPN highlights were playing on the big screen, but he wasn't paying it no mind, in fact, the T.V. was watching him. Truth reached inside the marble bowl sitting on the living room table and retrieved two big steel marbles. He rolled the marbles back and forth inside his palm while he meditated.

Truth was analyzing his life, the past and present. Prior to him jumping head first into the dope game, he had NBA dreams like any other teenager that played the game. Truth had a burning passion for the game of basketball. He spent countless hours working to perfect his skills. He would play with the old heads as much as possible then go in beast mode against kids his age.

Money was real tight in his household, so he cut hair to keep a few dollars in his pocket. After his mother was murdered, Truth's outlook on life changed. His heart turned ice cold. He couldn't understand why someone would want to harm his mother. She was the sweetest lady you could ever meet. His mother would feed the hungry kids in the neighborhood, even though they were barely getting by. The medical examiner autopsy report revealed that Truth's mother bled to death from eighteen puncture wounds to her heart and left for dead.

With no father figure present, Truth and his lil brother were left to fend for themselves at a young age. They stayed with their Aunt Lucille on the Eastside of Milwaukee, but she couldn't control them. Lucille had two kids of her own and barely had enough money to take care of herself. It was rough dealing with so much as a adolescent for Truth.

Truth reminisced on the day he first saw Rudy in his '91 Corvette with the top dropped. He was mesmerized by the beauty of the sportscar. Truth remembered envisioning himself behind the wheel of his own convertible. Rudy coached Victor Berger Warning Basketball Team. His whole team sported the latest Air Jordan's kicks, which matched their uniforms.

Rudy's team was stacked with the city's top prospects, and they were cocky ass hell. Truth thought about how he used to hoop in some hand me down Adidas Forums that curled up in the front, looking a hot mess. He wanted to be a part of Rudy's team so bad that the following summer he tried out for the team. Rudy actually had his team set, so even new people that tried out were likely to get cut regardless of how good they were.

Rudy's players were all going to a D-1 or 2 college. Truth hadn't made a name for himself among the cities top prospects, but niggaz in the hood respected his game. During tryouts Truth put on a clinic just to be cut later.

Truth was pissed he got cut. He thought his game spoke for itself, not to mention he wanted a free pair of Air Jordans. After being cut, he went back to his original team, "The Nad." He vowed to kill Rudy's team when they played against them and show him he made a major mistake cutting him.

During the course of the summer Truth developed a strong following. He torched teams left and right, playing with a vengeance. When the two teams met at North Division High School the gym was jam packed. Three other games were going on, but the crowd gathered in the stands to see who was gone kill who on the basketball court. Truth was relentless against Rudy's team. He brought his A- game out. He dished numerous pretty no-look passes to his teammates, bringing the crowd to their feet. Truth even dunked five times on Rudy's squad and made four three-pointers from downtown.

He laughed at Rudy's team each time he scored while tossing up the "E" reppin' his hood. Truth purposely looked Rudy's way every time he clowned his players. All Rudy could think was, That young nigga is the Truth. Immediately after that game, Rudy befriended Truth. He saw pro potential in him and figured now was the time to jump on the bus.

What Truth didn't know was Rudy used his players as dope runners. Eventually he earned his free pair of Air Jordan's, but he had to put in some work first. Truth became a dope runner and moved up fast in the rankings. After a year of running dope for Rudy, he realized Truth was a loyal worker and asset. Rudy decided to school him on all aspects of the dope game. Truth picked up fast. In no time he was in charge of one of Rudy's trap houses.

Truth wound up blowing his knee out in a pickup game hooping at Riverside High School and didn't go through with his rehab. He eventually called it quits on his hoop dreams and put his all into the dope game. Rudy tested Truth by playing mind games with him to see where his head was at. He would send his partners at Truth with lower dope prices to see if he would switch sides, he was solid. He never bit.

Once Rudy gave Truth a pistol with no bullets in it and staged a fake robbery to see if he'd bust. Truth passed every test he threw at him with flying colors. Truth lived up to his name in every way, but Rudy felt he couldn't let him get too powerful in the streets. He felt if he did, it would come a point where Truth wouldn't need him anymore. So Rudy fed Truth on a leash, not letting him excel to his full potential in the streets.

Truth, being street smart, peeped Rudy's lil game and started to despise him, which led to his demise.

"Truth!" Jazzie called out for the fifth time.

"Whuuut!" Truth yelled back as he quickly came back to reality.

"Take this phone, I done called yo' ass 'bout seven times!" Jazzie exaggerated as she handed Truth the cordless phone.

"I'm sorry shawty, I was deep in thought. Who is it?" Truth whispered as he covered the phone with his hand.

"Yo' grandma," she stated with an attitude.

"Oh, okay. Hey Granny," Truth greeted into the phone.

"Hey chile, I was just checking on you. I ain't want much," Truth's grandma stated in her syrupy southern drawl.

"Thanks Granny, I'm good. What about you?" He asked.

"You know these fools down hurr driving my ol' butt crazy, don't nobody got this or got that, just complain, complain, complain," she informed.

"You need anythang?" He asked, knowing the answer to his question.

"I'm a lil behind on a few bills," she explained.

"I'll send you a thousand dollars, is that cool?" He asked.

"Yes chile, bless yo' heart. You tell your brother to give me a call nah."

"I will Granny, don't be letting people stress you out, and tell errbody I said hi."

"Okay nah, tell yo' brother I said I love him too. Let me get on off dis phone, I love you."

"I love you too, Granny."

****

Boss, Trouble, and Truth went to Badger Gun Range for some target practice. Wawk! Wawk! Wawk! Wawk! Was the sound of the rounds as bullets ripped through their target sheets. They reloaded their guns, letting loose 'til all the shells emptied out of their magazines then stared at each other.

The three men were impressed with each other's accuracy. Surprisingly, they had a lot of head shots. The smell of gun smoke was intoxicating, but they were used to it. Visiting the gun range was a way to improve their tactical skills and relieve stress, plus find out what the new artillery was on the market. Whatever they didn't buy legally, they would purchase on the black market from their Arab connect.

"So how thangz goin' with dem niggaz up north?' Truth asked.

"Fam, off one brick I made 43 G'z fuckin' 'round with them niggaz. They be up in Green Bay and Oshkosh too. I'm just gone stick and move though. It ain't like the Mill, a nigga will be hot as a bitch pumping in those areas fo' too long. You still good though?"

"I believe I got a lil sumthin left, how you lookin', Trouble?"

"Mane cuz I'm good. I got enough to cop a whole brick, and my stash decent. When we gone party again?"

"I was thankin' 'bout throwing a party in Miami for my birthday. Since we havin' money now, itz time to do sum big boy shit," Truth announced as he gave Trouble and Boss dap.

"I'm with that!" Boss replied.

"I'll let yawl know something once I get tha details together, okay. But be prepared to have the time of yawl life, niggaz. I'm goin' in."

They all packed their equipment up then headed to their cars. Truth looked at his SS Impala thinking, Itz time to upgrade.

****

Joel Fletcher was consulting one of his clients when his phone rang.

"Would you please excuse me?" He stated softly.

Mr. Fletcher was one of the best defense attorneys in town. He was well-educated in corporate tax law and belonged to a prestigious law firm. In order to retain him, you had to be referred by one of his respected associates. Mr. Fletcher's retainer fee usually started off at $6,500. It just so happened Truth played in one of his basketball leagues when he was younger and developed a close relationship with Joel over the years.

Mr. Fletcher knew about Truth's past and what he was involved in. He tried to school him on how not to be the typical drug dealer. He was sick of seeing young black men risk their lives, and when they got busted not have anything to fall back on.

"Hello, Joel Fletcher speaking," he sang into the phone.

"Whuzz good Joel this Truth," Truth responded.

"Oh, what can I do for you, Truth?" Questioned the lawyer.

"First off, did you like that package I sent you?"

Truth was referring to the $20,000 he sent him on a retainer fee.

"Oh, yes I did," Joel responded with a smile.

"So now can I ask what can I do for you, Truth?"

Truth let out a little chuckle, "I'm thinking about renting a condo in Miami for my birthday and purchasing a car too, maybe a Benz. You got anyone you can refer me to?" Truth questioned.

Joel thought for a second before responding, "On the car, I can help you. I'll give my friend Jim Van Horn at Braman's Auto in Miami a call and let him know you're interested in purchasing a car. Oh! I have a friend who has a mansion she rarely uses, she travels in and out of the country a lot. I'll tell her I'm going to use it and to leave me the security code, but you gotta promise me you won't trash the place, Truth," Joel stated with hesitation.

"I got you Joel, simmer down, I wouldn't fuck you over like that," Truth swore.

"I see business been good for you, Truth."

"I can't complain," Truth replied with a slight grin.

"I think it's time we discuss business. I think I can help you prosper. Let's do lunch, you like Chinese food?" Joel asked.

"I love dat shit," Truth admitted.

"Good, meet me at Beni Hana at 1:30."

"I'll be thurr." Truth accepted.

Truth wondered what Joel had in mind, but figured whatever it was, it had to be good. Joel sat back in his fine Italian recliner chair and thought, If Truth was able to pay me $20,000 for a retainer fee and have enough money to buy a new Mercedes Benz, he had to have moved up in the drug game. It's time for me to introduce him to one of my biggest clients.

Joel Fletcher and Former Baseball Player, Sammy Ruiz, of the Milwaukee Brewers were good associates. Joel laundered money and made safe investments for Sammy Ruiz over the years. Unfortunately Joel made one bad decision on a business deal that cost Sammy a half million dollars. Ultimately Sammy expected

Joel to make it up to him since he guaranteed nothing would go wrong.

Joel was excited, because if he could hook Truth up with Sammy, he would gain Sammy's trust back and possibly have an extra line of credit for future investments.

"Helen, hold all my calls, I'm taking a late lunch," he instructed his receptionist.

"Okay Mr. Fletcher," Helen stated as she scribbled quickly on a pad of paper.

Joel Fletcher threw on his Armani sports jacket, grabbed his keys, briefcase, cell phone, then headed out the door. Truth was excited about the Mansion Joel plugged him with. He couldn't wait to tell Jazzie the news. Bzzz, Bzzz, Bzzz, Bzzzz, was the sound of Jazzie's cell phone.

"Hello," Jazzie greeted as she pushed her hair to the side.

"Hey Jaz."

Jazzie's face lit up after hearing Truth's voice.

"Hey Daddy!" She stated into the phone.

"It's a change of plans for my birthday, we going to Miami! Make sure you go shopping for some bikinis," he instructed her.

"You serious babe!" She asked.

Jazzie wasn't expecting a trip to Miami on such short notice.

"Serious as a heart attack," he laughed.

"Who all know about this?" Jazzie inquired.

"Nobody yet, but I gotta go. I got a meeting with my lawyer," he explained.

"Ok, I'll see you tonight then. I love you, Truth," she screamed with excitement.

"Love you too, bae," Truth shot back while laughing.

Truth pulled up to the valet at Beni Hana and tossed the overweight parking attendant his keys.

"Take care of her, bruh," Truth told the valet.

"Don't worry Sir, I will," the parking attendant responded.

Truth slid on his Cartier frames as he entered the restaurant. He was greeted by a maître d'.

"Dining by yourself today, Sir?" The host asked.

"No ma'am, I'm dining with a friend, Joel Fletcher. He should be expecting me," Truth replied, while glancing over the restaurant.

"Oh, right this way, Sir," the maitre d' stated politely as she led Truth to Joel's table.

Joel stood up to greet Truth with a firm handshake then took his seat.

"Would you like anything to drink, Sir?" The waitress asked.

"Yes, I would like a bottle of Chateau Haut Brion," Joel replied.

"I'll be right back with your bottle, by the way, nice selection."

Once the waitress was out of ear shot, the men began to talk.

"So whuz good, Joel?" Truth stated, getting right to the point.

"I think I can help you expand your business," Joel replied confidently.

Truth looked Joel directly into his eyes as the waitress returned with the bottle of wine.

"Are you two ready to place your orders?"

Joel always ordered the same thing, so he didn't need to view the menu.

"Yes, I'll take the Hibachi Steak entre, medium rare," Joel ordered.

"And you Sir?"

Truth was unsure of what he wanted, so he quickly scanned the menu.

"I'll take the Colossal Shrimp entre," he ordered.

"And would that complete your orders?" Questioned the waitress.

"Yes," they both replied simultaneously.

The waitress grabbed their menus then walked away.

"Now where were we, Truth?" Joel got right down to business.

"You mentioned being able to help my business expand," replied Truth.

"Ah, yes," Joel replied.

"Which business are you referring to, because I have several, Joel?" Truth stated seriously.

Joel filled their wine flutes up with wine then took a sip, savoring the taste before responding.

"The business that helped you acquire those businesses you now own," Joel pointed out.

"Oh okay," Truth replied with a grin.

"Let's cut to the chase, Truth. How much you paying per Kilo?" The lawyer asked flat out.

Truth was caught off guard by Joel's bluntness. He didn't want to say a number too high and mess up the chances of getting it much lower, so he thought precisely.

"Seventeen a key."

That was the first number he could think of that sounded realistic.

"Ah, I see you must've bought a lot to get those numbers?"

Truth squirmed around in his chair. He knew he couldn't let Joel see him sweat.

"What do you consider a lot?" He questioned the lawyer.

"Ten, fifteen Kilo's," Joel answered.

"You can say that," Truth responded, eager to see what his lawyer was up to.

"What if I tell you I can beat that price? How does fourteen sound to you? But you'll have to stop dealing with your supplier. That's the only catch," Joel proposed.

"Depends, is this a Milwaukee connect? I don't want nobody in town knowing my business, Joel," Truth explained.

"He's not here, so this will be a discreet venture. Actually, you won't have to meet him face to face," Joel assured.

Truth liked what he was hearing, but he didn't want Joel to think he was desperate.

"Well, when can I see a sample of the product?" He asked.

"After I talk to my source, I can have twenty kilo's shipped here by next week at the earliest. If you like what you see you can take them on consignment," Joel explained.

"I don't do fronts, Joel. That's punk shit," Truth informed Joel.

"Well in this world, you'll learn that some people will take that as an insult, turning down a good offer," Joel insinuated.

"So this is an offer?" Truth asked, looking for clarity.

Things had to be precise when it came to business.

"Consider it one my friend. Do you think I'd put you in a bad position? I know you have big dreams, and Milwaukee is too small for big dreams. I promise you if you stick with me, you'll achieve the inevitable," Joel promised.

"I'm already with you, Joel," Truth stated as he took a sip of the wine.

"One last thing, Truth," Joel interjected.

"Whuzz dat?" Asked Truth.

"Remember if you running a business don't be in the business, be on top of the business."

He wanted to make sure Truth knew this was a power move. Things start to get real when you cross over to big money.

"I like dat Joel, that's some inspirational shit," Truth replied.

"And something you should apply to your life. So can I proceed with this, and assume we have a deal?" Joel offered out his glass.

"You damn right."

They made a toast to becoming business partners. Truth couldn't believe his lawyer just plugged him with some bricks, and for a good price. Joel did the math in his head. Truth didn't know Joel was getting the bricks for ten G'z.

Ahh, eighty G'z would be my take for brokering this deal, Joel thought to himself as they ate their meals.

"Oh, I talked to my friend too, the Mansion is a go. Just let me know when you're going to Miami, and I'll give you the address and security codes."

He gave as many details as possible.

"Thanks Joel, what would I do without you?" Truth asked.

"That's a good question," Joel hinted as he cut into his steak.

Chapter 4

The annual Freak Fest was about to go down at Lincoln Park. The Freak Fest was Milwaukee's own version of Freaknic. The car wash, mall, hair and nail salon, barbershop, and stereo shop stayed busy on the day of the Freak Fest. Dudes were ready to pull out their prized whips. The women showed up half naked, wearing two piece swimsuits, ready to drop it like it's hot.

Jazzie and her entourage were dressed in red two-piece bathing suits, Chanel frames, Manolo heels, and their hair freshly whipped. They definitely stood out among the rest of the women who were starving for attention.

"Ewww, look at those bitches dancing on the hood of that car in thongs," Raquel pointed out as she turned her nose up in disgust.

"Bitch, that used to be us years ago, why you hating? They having fun the best way they know how," Jazzie stated, defending the young ladies.

"They still some lil tramps in my book," Raquel shot back.

"And what you think people use to say 'bout our hot asses?" Jazzie questioned.

"Bitch, shut up and pass the blunt," Raquel fussed as the girls burst out laughing.

They were enjoying the festivities while sitting on the trunk of Jazzie's Corvette. "Pop That Coochie" by Luke was blasting from somebody's trunk. The roars from motorcycles could be heard as they approached Lincoln Park parking lot. Heaven was leading the pack of bikers. She was on a black, blue, and yellow Kawasaki Ninja with a matching two piece bathing suit and all white Dukeys. There were various colors of motorcycles in Heaven's motorcade. The female bikers matched their bikes to the "T". When Heaven took off her helmet all eyes were on her, niggaz started gossiping like bitches. Heaven's two- piece appeared to be painted on her curvaceous body. Her skin glistened in the beaming sun like she had a whole bottle of baby oil on. Her legs were perfectly sculpted; her breasts sat up like they were at attention. Heaven was clearly the baddest bitch at Lincoln Park. They parked their bikes on the grass then walked towards the large crowd.

"Those hoes clownin'!" Raquel stated.

"They aight," Jazzie replied nonchalantly.

"They pulled up like some niggaz on them Ninja's. Them some Boss bitches. They make me want a motorcycle now," Raquel replied.

"So what you saying? We ain't Boss Bitches, Raquel? Them bitches ain't doing shit," Jazzie vented with an attitude.

"Nahh! I'm just giving them bitches they props, I dig they style," Raquel stated with defeat.

"It's called swagger, dummy," Jazzie shot back.

"I don't give a fuck what you call it, they got it goin' on," Raquel shot back as she twirled her fingers in the air.

"Whatever, let's go check out the dance contest," Jazzie stated, wanting to get out of Heaven's presence.

"Okay, but we gotta throw our purses in the trunk," Raquel uttered.

"Where did Alicia's ass go? Hoe must be out here looking for a trick," Jazzie joked.

"She might as well, we can't do shit. Errbody know who our niggaz are. We better represent too," Raquel emphasized.

"Damn, you so right bitch," Shana assured.

Four females were going at it, dancing like strippers to the song, "Do Do Brown." Money was raining over the exotic dancers as they pleased the crowd of horny men.

"Damn, her titties poppin' out her bra!" Someone yelled from the crowd.

The niggaz off Burleigh known as The Zoo started spraying Cristal over the dancers, getting the crowd geeked. Heaven tried to move out of the way and accidently bumped into Jazzie. Jazzie shot a menacing mean mug at Heaven.

"S'cuse you!" Jazzie barked angrily.

"I'm sorry, I didn't mean to bump into you," Heaven replied calmly.

"Next time look before you walk," Jazzie commanded.

"Damn! Why you so damn hostile? I already apologized to yo' ass," Heaven implied while mugging Jazzie back.

"Damn Jazzie, let that shit go. We tryna have a good time," Raquel insisted.

"You right Raquel, but I'll see you again, trick," Jazzie assured Heaven.

"And next time I bump into you, don't expect an apology. I hope you trained to go bitch," Heaven shot back as she stared Jazzie up and down, wondering what Truth saw in her.

"By the way Vic Tanny got a $19.99 membership special, you should go tighten yo' shit up," Heaven stated sarcastically.

Jazzie snatched her shoes off, Heaven got into her fighting stance. Their friends grabbed the both of them as they verbally assaulted each other. The intoxicated crowd turned their attention towards the women.

Somebody yelled, "Cat Fight!"

"Let me go! Raquel, let's beat these bitches ass!" Jazzie hollered furiously.

Instantly it was on between both entourages. Homer Blow and Reggie Brown grabbed their bullhorns when they saw what was happening.

"Somebody break that shit up before the Sheriffs get here and shut us down!"

Niggaz from the Eastside grabbed Jazzie and her crew, while the niggaz from Westlawn grabbed Heaven and her crew. Fortunately nobody was seriously injured.

"This the reason we barely got Afro Fest and Juneteenth Day! Before you know it, that's gone be cut down to a one block celebration!" Homer Blow yelled from his bull horn.

The crowd was in complete silence. Homer Blow was well-respected in the community, so the crowd calmed down knowing he was speaking the truth. The music came back on once the situation was under control. Once the bootys started popping, everybody seemed to forget about the incident except the ladies.

Big Dog drove his '96 Suburban over the grass towards the crowd then flung his doors open. He was beating, "Dusted and Disgusted," by E-40. The ground vibrated from the four fifteen-inch Strokers. The bass was hitting so hard the truck looked like it was taking deep breaths. He had two 6 ½ inch Clarion Speakers in each door, two 6x9 Clarion Speakers in the dash, and 10 MB Polk tweeters scattered throughout the truck to help bring a crisp sound inside.

A bump out started as niggaz started popping their trunks. Tim Dog's Chevy conversion van was the only thing able to compete with Big Dog Suburban. STim Dog had four 18inch Kicker competition woofers in his van and eight Pioneer 350 watts 6x9's placed throughout. The Freak Fest was going down in a major way until someone left the park, ran a red light on Green Bay and Hampton then had an accident.

With tempers flaring, a fight broke out between the people involved in the accident. Police swarmed the scene, trying to control the crowd as fists and bottles flew through the air.

"Everybody please vacate the park! This is a direct order! Those who choose to disobey will be arrested for trespassing and public intoxication!" Yelled the Sheriff's from their bullhorn.

People hauled ass trying to get away. Some niggaz had warrants and were packing heat and wasn't trying to go to jail.

"These niggers never get along when they get together," one of the white Sheriffs uttered to a fellow Sheriff.

"They keep it up there won't be an African World Festival left, dumb fuckers." The older of the two stated.

He had seen this type of behavior so many times at these events. The Sheriffs knew there would be problems way before it started.

****

Joel Fletcher boarded a Red Eye flight to Los Angeles, California. His flight arrived at L.A.X five hours later. Cecil, Sammy's top lieutenant, greeted Joel Fletcher warmly then chauffeured him off to Sammy Ruiz' estate in a black H1 Hummer.

"How was your flight, Senor Fletcher?" Cecil inquired in his rich Spanish accent.

"Rather comfortable Cecil," Joel replied modestly.

"Mr. Ruiz will be happy to see you. Will you be staying with us for awhile?" The Cecil questioned.

"I'm sorry Cecil, I won't be here long. I'm only here on business. I have to be back in Milwaukee tomorrow," Joel replied.

"Oh, I see. Well, I hope you enjoy your short stay, but if you decide to stay a bit longer, I'd love to take you to our newest establishment. I guarantee you'll love it," Cecil stated as he winked his left eye at Joel.

"I'll make sure I take you up on that offer next time I'm in town."

The Hummer navigated through the California traffic like the president was inside. The weather was absolutely beautiful, not a cloud in the sky. Joel gazed up at the panoramic roof, admiring the scenery. I need to get out of Milwaukee more often, he thought.

Sammy Ruiz was one of the biggest cocaine and arms distributors on the West Coast. He owned two shopping malls, one in Beverly Hills, one in Miami, an electric company, a wine vineyard, and stocks in various fortune 500 corporations. Sammy was born in Chitre, Panama and was treated like a King whenever he visited. He made sure he gave back to the poor, mainly because he remembered how hard it was for him growing up in a two bedroom shack, with four brothers and three sisters, barely eating on the daily, let alone having the proper clothing to attend school.

As a National Baseball Player Sammy was named an All-star three times before he was banned from the league for testing positive for steroid use. Over the years, Sammy developed a reputation in the drug underworld for being a ruthless, callous dictator. Whenever someone came up short with his money, Sammy wouldn't kill that person, he would have their family touched.

Sammy handled things that way so the person that crossed him would have to suffer for the rest of their life knowing they sacrificed their family over money.

As they pulled up to the estate, they were greeted by a ten foot tall steel security gate. Two burly brown skinned Dominican men with long ponytails, dressed in black suits, and wearing earpieces approached the Hummer carrying M-16 rifles.

"How are you today, Senor Cecil," one of the big goons greeted.

"Good, good," Cecil responded.

"Mr. Ruiz is expecting you and Mr. Fletcher." The head security guard uttered.

Cecil nodded his head keeping the conversation short. The steel gates slowly opened, allowing the guests to enter the gorgeous estate. After they parked the massive truck, they were greeted by two beautiful ladies resembling super models of Latin decent. The ladies were dressed in two-piece bathing suits with matching heels. Their bodies were sculpted like the number eight, with toffee toned skin. Sammy had to have the best of everything at all times.

"Hello Senor Cecil, Mr. Ruiz is on the golf course. I'll take you and your friend to meet him," one of the ladies stated.

"Why thank you Senorita," Cecil replied.

As they drove to the golf course, Joel flirted with the females forcing them to giggle. Mr. Ruiz was a terrible golfer, but people would purposely loose to him in fear of what the repercussions might be.

As they approached Sammy, all that could be seen was a cloud of sand flying everywhere. Sammy was definitely frustrated. Cecil and Joel stepped off the golf cart headed towards Sammy's. Sammy stopped swinging his golf club as he gaped at Joel and

Cecil walking towards him. He wiped the beads of sweat off his forehead with his glove.

"Joel buddy! Long time no see, huh?" Sammy shouted as he hugged Joel.

"Is that a good or bad thing, Sammy?" Joel replied as he released his arms from Sammy's tight grip.

"Depends on the situation," Sammy stated with a grin.

"How's business in Milwaukee?" Sammy asked.

"Fine, in five more years I'll be ready to retire, probably move next door to you so I can teach you how to play golf," Joel joked.

"Ha, Ha, Ha, you're pretty funny, Joel. We party in Cali. Do you think you can handle living here?" Sammy stated sarcastically.

"I'm only thirty-five, I got a lot of life left in this body, my friend," Joel shot back.

"So what brings you to the City Of Angels? You running from something?" Sammy insinuated with one eye arched.

"Who me? I'm Joel Fletcher, I run from no man," Joel replied confidently.

"Well come on, what is it? Spit it out my friend."

"Can we at least have some privacy to discuss business?"

Sammy clapped his hands, uttered something in Spanish and the ladies left their presence. Cecil escorted Sammy and Joel over to the Olympic sized pool so they could discuss business in a relaxing setting.

"You care for something to drink, my friend?" Sammy asked Joel.

"Scotch would be fine." Joel responded.

Sammy motioned for his maid Catalina. The elderly Dominican woman quickly came to their service.

"What can I do for you, Senor Ruiz?" Catalina inquired in her thick Spanish accent.

"Please bring a dry Scotch for my friend," Sammy instructed.

"Si Senor."

The young woman left the men to talk. Sammy lit a Cuban cigar savoring the smell and texture as he passed the box of cigars to Joel.

"No thanks Sammy, those things are going to be the death of you," Joel stressed as he placed the box on the table.

"See, that's where you're wrong. Twenty year old pussy is gone be the death of me," Sammy replied as him, and Cecil burst out laughing.

Catalina returned with the drink. Sammy smiled at her as she handed it to Joel.

"Thank you Catalina," Sammy stated.

"Will you be needing anything else, Senor?" Catalina inquired in a soft tone.

"No darling, your services are appreciated."

"Thank you Senor Ruiz."

Joel downed the Scotch, then wiped his mouth with his hand.

"So tell me Joel, how can I help you?" Sammy asked seriously.

Joel cracked his knuckles, swayed his head from side to side then cleared his throat.

"One of my clients need a strong coke connect, and since I trust him, I figured I'd broker a deal between you and him."

Sammy took a puff of his cigar then blew smoke rings into the air.

"Ahh, I love Cuban cigars. So is this client of yours, someone I know?" Sammy questioned.

"No, he's up and coming in Milwaukee. I've been coaching him on how to stay invisible on the streets, and he's doing pretty damn good," Joel informed.

"So what do you want from me? He can't score in Milwaukee?" Sammy questioned, with a brow raised.

"We want your grade of coke, and plus, I'm trying to squash the debt I have with you. My guy is moving a lot of weight." Joel confessed.

Sammy studied Joel's face. He still remembered the loss he took with their last investment. He was a bit reluctant to deal with Joel.

"How much coke do you need?" Sammy asked, getting right to the point.

Joel dropped his head then gazed at Sammy.

"For now, twenty kilo's," Joel stated proudly.

"Ahhh, so you're really serious?" Sammy uttered as he dumped his cigar ashes on the ground.

"Yes Sammy. Do you think I'd come this far for the hell of it?" He questioned.

"Of course not Joel, I tell you what, I'll send you ten kilos by Cecil in a few days at ten K a piece just to see how fast your client can move them. Make sure you report to me in a couple weeks, and remember, you co-signed for this guy Joel, so don't let me down, okay?"

Sammy figured he'd give Joel whatever he needed. That way he could see a return on his loss.

"Well, this meeting is adjourned. Let's go inside and play with the Senorita's!" Sammy blurted as he rose from his patio chair.

"I'll stay for a few more hours, but I gotta Red Eye back tonight, Sammy."

"Fucking party pooper," Sammy joked as he slapped Joel on the shoulder.

They ran into the massive seven bedroom mansion, anticipating the fun they were about to have with the beautiful ladies. Life was definitely wonderful at the top.

****

Bzzz, Bzz, Bzzz, Bzzz, was the sound of Truth's cell phone as it danced on his bedroom dresser.

"Hello," Truth answered groggily.

"Hey buddy, this is Joel."

Truth wiped the sleep from his eye as he rose up.

"Whuzz zatnin?" He asked.

"I got some good news," Joel exclaimed.

"Bring it on then," Truth was at full attention.

"Well, our business venture is finalized. We will be up and running in a few days, so don't make any plans, okay," Joel directed.

"Huh bruh, thatz all good, thanks Joel!" Truth replied ecstatically.

"No problem, I gotta look out for my friends," Joel returned.

"Can't wait to see those white bitches," Truth exclaimed with excitement.

"Ohh believe me, you're about to be a rich man." Joel assured Truth as he grinned.

"Talk to you later, Truth. I'm about to board my flight," Joel concluded.

"Ok, bruh."

After ending the call with Truth Joel smiled, he was in high spirits since he stood to make money hand over fist off Truth.

Chapter 5

Woo was a young teen who lived on the block and dreamed of being down with Truth but never earned a spot. He had animosity with Trouble since Truth handed the block over to him. Woo grew up on the Eastside and figured he was next in line. Truth didn't trust Woo due to the fact that he was a powder head. There was no way he was going to put his trust in a fiend.

Woo had an expensive nose candy habit. He was barely copping a half an ounce and kept falling off. He would blow everyone under the table at the aftersets, and when the powder ran out, he'd shake everybody down to see who was holding out on him. Woo's street resume held no credibility. Those facts alone were the reason Truth didn't respect Woo, nor trust him. A real hustler knew, "All money ain't good money."

As far as Truth knew nobody in his squad powdered their nose. If they did they were immediately removed from the clique and barred from hustling in the hood. One day Woo grew some superman balls and decided to tip on Trouble's block, why he decided to do that was a question none of the fiends could answer.

****

Trouble was dry. He was waiting on Truth to re-up so he hopped in traffic, heading to Bouchard's to do some shopping.

"Let me get seven pair of different colored Dukey's in a size 9 ½, Jim," Trouble requested as he looked around to see who was paying attention to him getting his stunt on.

"Gotcha, you see all the new authentic jerseys we got in? They'll go good with the Dukeys, Trouble," The cashier offered.

"Mane, if you cut me a deal I'll cop a few. I really wanted a few of those Nike Golf Polos, bruh," Trouble replied.

"We got you, and I'm gone throw a few fitted hats in too," The man stated.

"Good looking out, bruh, you always keep a nigga fitted when I come through," Trouble admitted as he rubbed his hands in a circular motion. Trouble's cell phone started vibrating, so he cut the conversation short with Jim. "Who dis?" Trouble spoke.

"This Tammy, you gave Woo permission to slang on the block? If not, he in front of yo' spot getting it in," the dopefiend confessed as she scratched her head.

"Hell nawl! Tell that bitch I'ma be to see his ass for disrespecting me like dat!" Trouble barked through the phone. "Matter of fact, don't say shit, I got a surprise fo' his bitch ass," Trouble replied with a grin.

Trouble loved drama, that's how he earned the name Trouble. He didn't play when it came to niggaz disrespecting. His name meant the world to him. He felt if you disrespected him in any way you was ready to go to war, and he was TTG "trained to go" at all times.

"You straight JaBar?" Trouble asked.

"Yeah bruh."

JaBar was Trouble's goon from his hood in Louisiana. He sent for him once everything checked out in the Mill. JaBar was trained to go as well. Trouble took him under his wings at the tender age of thirteen. His mother was strung out on heroine and would disappear for days, leaving him to fend for himself. JaBar had so much love for Trouble he was willing to sacrifice his life for him. One night Trouble crept by one of his rival's girlfriend's house after the club closed and fucked her brains out. He was knocked out cold when suddenly he heard someone trying to gain entrance.

"Who the fuck is that, bitch!" Trouble snapped as he reached for his pistol.

"I think itz my baby daddy, he the only one that got keys to my house," Kia mumbled shamefully.

"Fuck! This shit fucked up!" Trouble stated angrily.

"What you worried 'bout, fool? He can't get in hurr, I locked all the locks. He only got a key to the front door. Plus, that nigga on parole. He knows I'll call his P.O. on his weak ass," Kia lied, acting like she had no love for her baby daddy.

"Bitch you geeked! That nigga coming for my head. He seen my car out front, plus, you got all the locks on the front door. That mane know you in hurr fuckin'. I advise yo' ass to hit the floor now, because it's 'bout to get ugly in dis bitch," Trouble stated clearly as he picked his pistol up from the floor.

"What you tryna say, Trouble? You ain't finna do no shooting round here," Kia got up to stop Trouble from destroying her home.

"Bitch fuck you! You already know how I get down. I ain't 'bout to get killed over nann bitch pussy."

He pushed her to the side. Trouble took his pistol off safety then peeked out the window. He peeped his enemy going under his seat. He already knew what the deal was from their last encounter. He knew gunplay was definitely going to erupt. Trouble's choices were limited at this point, either he would stay inside and die like a bitch, or come out dumping. Being against all odds was something Trouble had been too familiar with. The longer he sat, the more his blood began to boil.

Instead of waiting for his rival to bring the drama, Trouble decided to bomb first. He crept out of the rear of the house, crouched down on one knee and opened fire. Trouble's Glock 40 was clearly no match against the goon's arsenal. Trouble was down to his last bullet when suddenly JaBar ran up shooting back recklessly with a AK-47.

Trouble took cover as the Ak-47 bullets ripped through everything in their path. The gun battle lasted for two minutes before Trouble's rival hauled ass. Once the smoke cleared, Trouble and JaBar fled the scene like thieves in the night. From that day forth Trouble kept JaBar by his side. When he ate, they both ate. Trouble felt he owed JaBar for saving his life.

****

JaBar balled out, he had at least five bags filled with the latest gear. Trouble made sure he took good care of JaBar like Truth blessed him.

"Oh Jim, let me get a pair of Havana Joe's and a Coogi, I want something exclusive, bruh," Trouble rattled off.

"Damn Trouble, you breaking the bank today, huh? When the fall Pelle' Pelle' jackets come in I'm calling you first," Jim promised as he walked behind the counter to ring up Trouble's items.

"So whatz my total, Jim?" Trouble asked.

Jim rang everything up quickly then grinned.

"$3500, would've been $4000, but I gave you my discount."

Trouble reached inside his Gucci bag and tossed Jim four bundles of money, each holding a grand.

"Keep the change bruh," Trouble stated as he reached for his bags.

"I appreciate it, Trouble. I told you I got you when the new shipment of Pelle' Pelle's come in," Jim reminded.

"No doubt, I know you got a nigga." Trouble and JaBar grabbed their bags then exited the store. "Say JaBar peep this shit out, Woo in front of the spot catching, bruh. Can you believe the nerve of that bitch ass nigga!" Trouble roared angrily.

"He must thank itz sweet or sumthin, bruh." JaBar shot back with a scowl.

Trouble popped in Master P's "Ice Cream Man" CD then skipped to his favorite song, "'Bout it 'bout it." His black 1969 Cutlass Supreme 442 was in mint condition. It was sitting on 16 inch Chrome Dayton's wrapped in low profile Vogue tires.

Trouble reached into his ashtray for the piece of blunt he hadn't finished. He stuck the flame to the blunt, took a hard drag then passed it to JaBar.

"Bruh, Woo gone have to pay for disrespecting me like that, on errthang. I hope his momma prayed for his ass when she woke up this morning cuz I ain't playing with dat fuck boy," Trouble stated.

"Huh bruh! That fuck nigga gone learn today!" JaBar snapped, ready for anything.

Trouble stepped on the gas, his glass packs roared like a pride of angry lions. The Cutlass trunk was beating out of control, like gorillaz trying to bust out of it. Niggaz in the hood didn't feel their whips were complete until they slapped a loud ass system in their cars. Trouble pulled over by a beat-up powder blue 1993 Chevy Cavalier he kept parked a few blocks away from his trap house then popped the hood.

He searched his glove box for something to use to scrape some battery acid off the battery post. After finding an old pair of tweezers, he started scraping the battery post. He scooped the tan powdery acid inside a sandwich bag and tied it tight. It looked like he had about a gram of real cocaine inside the baggie. Trouble grinned as he stuffed the bag inside his underwear.

Trouble sent a fiend to cop a couple P's from Woo to mix in with the battery acid to better disguise it. Minutes later him and JaBar pulled up on 1st N. Palmer and spotted Woo catching sales right in front of the house, exactly as dope fiend Tammy reported. Trouble pulled up in front of his trap house with the music bumping so loud people started dancing in the middle of the street and staring out their windows. Woo heard Trouble before he turned the corner, but he didn't run. He wanted Trouble to see what he was doing.

Trouble pulled in front of the traphouse grinning as he slapped his whip into park.

"Whuzz zatnin whoaday!" Trouble uttered while flashing his gold teeth.

"Not much East," Woo replied calmly. "Chill with that East shit, bruh. I'm from the boot," Trouble shot back.

"Damn, my bad nigga," Woo apologized. "Don't trip bruh, I was just saying."

JaBar was itching to burn Woo with a hot bullet, but he knew he had to wait on Trouble to get the green light.

"We got some new shit in, bruh, Peruvian flake too, my nig. You wanna blow?" Trouble offered with a mischievous look on his face.

The thought of coating his nose with some Peruvian flake made Woo drop his guard and take Trouble up on his offer. Woo thought about the free high. He knew Trouble was getting money and would probably set out an 8ball.

"You know I don't turn down shit but my collar, Fam." Woo admitted as he slowly approach Trouble's whip.

"Well, get in then. We can hit a few corners, blow, and get at some bitches!" Trouble stated, trying to bait Woo in.

Trouble smashed the gas, smoking the block up, while JaBar hung out the window bobbing his head to the music.

"This that shit my nigga, straight from Columbia, I don't thank you ready fo' dis hurr, bruh," Trouble proclaimed while grinning.

"Nigga, my nose like a vacuum cleaner. I done tooted with the best of them, Folks," Woo stressed while rubbing his nostrils.

"Stop at the liquor store on Holton, bruh, so I can buy a bottle," JaBar commanded.

Trouble dipped in front of a car, pulled in front of the liquor store then cut the ignition.

"Bring us back a fifth of Yac, bruh," Trouble stated while grinning at JaBar.

JaBar exited the car with a smile on his face, leaving Trouble and Woo in the car by themselves. Woo was a bit nervous, he wondered why Trouble hadn't spoke about him slanging in front of his traphouse.

"You ain't tryna off the Cutty, mac nigga?" Woo asked, trying to break the silence.

"Give me ten G's, it's yearns," Trouble replied as he looked over his shoulder at Woo.

"Damn nigga, you taxing fo' this bitch," Woo replied.

"I got twenty G's in it easy, bruh." Trouble turned the ignition then gunned the gas a few times. "Listen to this bitch growl, bruh!" VRMMM, VRMM, VRMMM, was the sound of the glass packs as they hollered. "You hurr dat shit, nigga? Don't act like you don't know how a snot whip sound," Trouble demonstrated.

"Nah folks, I was just saying that's too rich for my blood," Woo replied.

"Whatever, cheap ass nigga."

JaBar passed Trouble the fifth of Hennessy as he entered the car. Trouble blessed the bottle then passed it to Woo.

"Kill that shit nigga, ain't no bitches up in hurr!" Trouble persuaded Woo while grinning,

"You ain't said shit, Folks!" Woo shot back as he turnt the bottle of Hennessy up, took a big swig, then passed it back to Trouble. "Whut up with some of that white girl my nigga, sprinkle me," Woo stated as he wiped his nostrils as if it was dripping snot or something.

"Oh damn, I almost forgot 'bout that, bruh. Nigga, take it easy too, this that flaky flake, save some fo' us too, greedy nigga." Trouble had a sneaky smirk on his face, knowing him and JaBar didn't powder their nose.

Woo took the bag of powder, untied the knot, dipped his pinky finger into the bag then stuck his finger up his right nostril. Woo quickly coated the other nostril with the powdery substance, trying to be greedy. Immediately the lining of his nostrils started to burn, Woo thought he was snorting Peruvian flake. He had no idea he had just snorted battery acid laced with cocaine. As Trouble pulled off, he cranked his music up to the max then started bobbing his head. JaBar gazed over at him with a devilish grin. Trouble smiled then mumbled something under his breath.

Once the acid penetrated Woo's bloodstream, he started to convulse and shake uncontrollably in the backseat. Woo grabbed

Trouble by the shoulder with all his strength. JaBar slapped Woo with brute force, trying to break his grip.

"Bruh, did you really think shit was that sweet with us? Niggaz from the South don't play, bruh!" JaBar snapped.

"Oh, that was battery acid yo' thirsty ass just snorted too, bruh! I could've pushed yo' shit back, but that was too easy. I wanted to watch yo' bitch ass die slow," Trouble snickered as Woo became weak.

Woo's body jerked violently, his eyes were bucked like he saw a ghost. His life flashed before his eyes, and for the first time in his life, he felt helpless. He had gotten away with a lot of dirt over the years, and now he was paying the ultimate price, karma finally caught up to him. He always thought he'd go out in a blaze and take a few people with him. He couldn't believe he got outsmarted the way he did.

Foam poured out of Woo's mouth like a soda being shook up, then opened. Seconds later his heart collapsed as he released his bowels. It was almost check out time for poor Woo. Trouble and JaBar rushed over to an abandoned house on the opposite side of town to dispose of the body. Trouble parked in the back so no one would see them dragging the body.

JaBar poured the bottle of Hennessy over Woo's body then struck a match, setting him ablaze. The house slowly erupted into violent flames that spread throughout each room. The house slightly glowed in a fluorescent orange border, the neighbors ran outside to witness the horrible scene. Trouble fled the scene like a bat out of hell heading towards his storage space to ditch his car.

"JaBar, we can't tell Truth bout this. You know he'll snap." Trouble instructed.

"Bruh, I'm already knowing," Jabar agreed.

"If anybody ask about Woo, just tell 'em we dropped him off at the liquor store. We can't deny seeing him. I know somebody seen him hopping in the whip," Trouble stated nervously.

"Don't trip Troub, the nigga would've still been alive if he wasn't on that fuck shit," JaBar pointed out.

"Well, I bet nann nother nigga pull no fuck shit like that again," Trouble promised.

Once the hood got a whiff of what just took place, Trouble and JaBar would be the first names to come to mind. Bad news always traveled fast. Depending on your status in the hood no one cared about what happened to you, especially if that person was on everyone's hit list.

Trouble wanted to send a message to the streets. He was stressing that they are not to be played with or disrespected in any form or fashion. Trouble and JaBar were about that gun play all day 24/7. They welcomed anybody that wanted to test their nuts.

****

"Boss, you ready to get dis money, bruh?" Truth spoke into the phone.

"Man, you know I been waiting on yo' slow ass to reup! I'm ready to feed the streets and get to this paper, Folks!" Boss voiced anxiously.

"I just got the green light so errthang a go, Fam, we in now. I hope you still stackin' yo' cheese, bruh, cuz after a few good runs I'm getting out this shit," Truth warned Boss.

"Yeah right muhfucka! The fuck you gone do then?"

"I don't know yet."

"Nigga, you getting too much paper to just walk away from this game. You can tell that bullshit to somebody else, I ain't tryna hear it," Boss objected, not believing a word Truth just said.

"I'm fo' real bruh, on my mom's grave, may she rest in peace, I'm not hustling for the rest of my life. You can't be a black millionaire in Milwaukee and think you gone be able to spend yo' dirty money. The Feds gone be ready to take a look at a nigga. Look at what happened to J-Dub," Truth explained.

"I feel what ya saying, East, but I heard somebody told on him from his clique. We ain't cut like that, Folks," Boss chipped in.

"Okay, I feel you on that note, but who's to say that can't happen to us?' Truth elaborated, raising the reason of doubt.

Boss pondered for a second. He wasn't sure if he should be taking Truth serious or not.

"True, true, but I'm just saying, if we ever go down I'm sure errbody gone hold their own weight," Boss stressed as he looked away from Truth.

"I'm pretty sure we all will. Matter fact, letz just change the subject before we jinx ourselves, bruh." Truth stated, ready to make money.

"Aight go ahead and change the subject ol' paranoid ass nigga," Boss joked.

"Fam, on some real shit, I'm tryna plan our future so we can kick our feet up and live stress free. Whatever I do, you know I'm gone include you in, bruh," Truth assured Boss.

"I'm already knowing Folks, so what you thinking bout doing?" Boss asked, focusing all his attention towards Truth.

"I gotta invest in Future. That nigga talented as fuck, he gone make us legit millionaires in the music industry. I was thinking about opening up a stereo shop and a club, but I know somebody will fuck my shit up," Truth admitted.

"Maaaaan, who you telling? That's why we ain't got but a few places to go as it is, hatin' ass, broke niggaz always fuckin' shit up. Mark my word, C.C.'s gone be the next spot to get closed down," Boss stated.

"So much shit be happening up thurr," Truth agreed.

"The stereo shop sounds like a good idea though, Truth. I know there is a vacant building on 14th N North," Boss told his partner.

"Damn, you sure right bruh, and Heaven a realtor, I can have her holla at the owner and see what they asking to lease that mudda fucka. I see you got yo' thinking cap on, East," Truth stated while nodding his head.

"I see what you on, Truth, now let's concentrate on feeding the streets, fam."

"Fo sho Boss, matter fact, after I holla at my people, we should hook up at Lincoln Park and throw some meat on the grill," Truth insisted.

"I'm with that, Folk. Is Jazzie throwing down on the grill?" Boss asked.

"You already know it, bruh. I'll call Trouble and let dem know we bar-b-queing later."

"Aight, do that and holla at me when those thangs on deck. I got niggaz waiting on me."

"I gotcha bruh," Truth assured Boss before ending the call.

"Jazzie, won't you run to Pick 'N Save and grab some meat. We 'bout to throw a bar-b-que up at Lincoln!" Truth yelled from the living room.

Jazzie was busy doing her toenails and talking on the phone with Raquel.

"You want me to go now!" Jazzie hollered back at Truth.

"Yup, so you might as well stop what you doing!"

Jazzie shook her head then hissed, "Girl, let me get off this phone and run to Pick 'N Save. Truth is throwing a bar-b-que up at Lincoln, make sure you bring yo' ass up there too," Jazzie insisted.

"I'll be there. I'll catch a ride with Boss," Raquel replied.

"Aight, I guess I'll see you then." Jazzie concluded.

After ending the call, Jazzie headed towards the living room to talk to Truth.

"Who gone do all the cooking?" Jazzie asked as she placed her hand on her hip.

"Shiiiidd, we is," Truth grinned.

"We huh? Every time you plan a bar-b-que, yo' ass will start off helping then creep off," Jazzie complained as she poked her mouth out and flung her head to the side.

"Well, today gone be different, I'ma put some work in, babe. Nnow come hurr and give me sum suga'."

Jazzie blushed as Truth sucked on her juicy lips and palmed her apple shaped behind. Jazzie felt like the luckiest woman on earth. Only if Law was like this with me, thought Jazzie.

"Don't start nothing you can't finish, Truth," Jazzie moaned.

"Get yo' ass on to the grocery store then, gurl."

He released his grip on her.

"Aight. Give me yo' keys and some money, 'cause you know I can't fit no groceries in the Vet." Truth tossed Jazzie a book of food stamps. "Are you serious? Food stamps nigga?" Jazzie stated with disgust.

"What? That shit spends like real money," Truth shot back. Jazzie mugged Truth as she snatched the food stamps and walked out the door. "I love you too bae, and make sure you bring back some Peanut Butter Captain Crunch," Truth joked.

"Fuck you," Jazzie whispered under her breath as she shut the door.

****

Detective Bryant was in the dog house with his wife since his suspension. His wife couldn't get over the fact that he cheated on her with a prostitute. She couldn't stand the sight of him. Whenever he was near her, the skin on her neck would cringe.

Detective Bryant was barred from their bedroom and forced to sleep on the couch. Not only was he forced to sleep on the couch, his wife was giving him the silent treatment. Mentally Detective Bryant was falling apart. He wasn't keeping up with his personal hygiene and started drinking heavily.

"How can my life get any worse than this?" He sobbed.

Seconds later his wife entered the living room with bags under her eyes like she had been crying all night.

"I want a divorce, I can't do this anymore! You totally embarrassed me and our family. I don't want anything to do with your trifling ass!" Martha shouted.

"Please honey, don't do this to me now! You're all I have, I can't live without you!" Detective Bryant pleaded.

"You should've thought about that when you were out screwing prostitutes, you selfish bastard!" Martha stately coldly.

"I'm sorry honey, what more can I say or do?" Detective Bryant cried.

"You damn right you're sorry! I'm sorry I ever married your no good trifling ass!"

Martha stormed out of the house, leaving him on his hands and knees. Detective Bryant was in shock. He couldn't imagine not having Martha and his son, in his life. At that moment he wanted revenge on the thugs that fucked his life up sending it to shambles.

****

Truth and Jazzie found a spot where they could set up, then unloaded the food. Truth was hands on with the grilling, proving Jazzie wrong. Everyone showed up for the bar-b-que. Raquel, Trouble, JaBar, Boss, and a few of their closet associates, were all engaging in conversation and having a great time.

Everything was going smooth as they popped bottle after bottle. Before they knew it, Lincoln Park's parking lot was littered with people coming from the lake front. When they saw all the cars in the parking lot, people knew Lincoln was the place to post up.

"Can I have all of y'all attention please!" Truth commanded. "Just so everybody know, my birthday is next month and I'm throwing a party in Miami and errbody hurr is invited. So bitches, get yo' two-pieces together, and niggaz get ready to party! We leaving the haters behind with dey monkey asses!" Truth announced.

The crowd was geeked, they started whistling and talking about the party amongst themselves.

"Should I invite Heaven since she helped me with my businesses?" Truth pondered.

"Cuz, you clownin' mane, is Future gone be at the party? I ain't seen that nigga in a minute," Trouble asked, hoping the answer would be yes.

"Of course he gone be thurr, bruh. One mo' thang before I forget y'all, itz gone be an all white party!" Truth informed the crowd.

The cook out was a success. Jazzie was pleased Truth kept his word and didn't leave her hanging. Truth took a seat on the park bench away from everyone else. He signaled for his head lieutenant Boss and Trouble to come join him. He took a bite of his bratwurst then cracked open a Corona.

Bees started to hover over him, causing him to drop his Bratwurst as he swatted his paper plate, trying to drive them away.

"Fuck! Damn bees!" Truth snapped.

Boss walked up giggling at Truth. He found it amusing seeing a grown ass man running from an insect.

"I see you out here attracting bees and shit, my nigga," Boss teased Truth while taking a seat on the park bench.

"These muhfuckas tried to hoe me out my beer and brat, folks," Truth whined.

Trouble and Boss looked at each other then burst out laughing. Truth continued to swat at the bees. He really got pissed when he spilled his beer on his Polo shirt.

"Damn! Let's move to another table. These bees pissing me the fuck off!" Trouble and Boss still had smirks on their faces as they followed Truth to another park bench. "Here's the deal y'all, the shipment is supposed to be in tomorrow, so don't make any plans. If this shit turn out to be butta, then we in tha game. The prices real sweet too, so a nigga can really eat," Truth stressed to his squad.

"Good looking folks, I already like the sounds of this," Boss concurred with a big smile.

"Well, drink up and enjoy the food, my gurl already mad I got her slaving over the grill, that's all I had to tell y'all."

Boss and Trouble stood up and were about to walk off. Truth tapped Trouble on the shoulder, stopping him in his tracks. Boss stopped then looked back wondering what Truth was on.

"Go ahead Boss, let me holla at cuz real quick," Truth stated.

"Errthang good?" Boss questioned.

"Fo sho, ain't nothing you should be worried about, bruh," Truth insisted.

"Aight East."

Trouble could sense a problem. Boss continued on as Truth directed his attention towards Trouble.

"Whutz hatnin' cuz?" Trouble asked.

"I know 'bout that homi y'all did, all I gotta say is good job. Next time, don't be so fast to bust a nigga head open without running it through me. If we start stacking bodies up round hurr the Feds gone be to see us, so use yo' head next time."

Trouble looked down towards the ground.

"I feel you big cuz, I just did what I thought you'd do," Trouble admitted.

"I probably would've did the same thang, just remember drugs and murder will bring down any empire, cuz. We in this to get rich, thatz it," Truth explained.

"Gotcha cuz, next time I'll check with you before I body a nigga. I just can't stand it when a weak ass nigga try me, you know how we get down in the LP," Trouble expressed.

"I'm already knowing cuz, Milwaukee way different than Lake Providence. This a dead conversation, Cuz, letz go smash some bar-b-que," Truth stated.

Truth smiled at Trouble. He loved the fact that Trouble was pure gangsta and wouldn't let anyone walk over him, but he knew drugs and murders didn't mix in no city. He couldn't help laughing at Trouble for his last comment, he gave Trouble some dap thinking, I love this nigga.

They continued to party and congregate until the park's lights came on. As the crowd started to leave, Truth found some kids to help clean up the mess they made and paid them twenty-five dollars a piece for their services. The kids were happy with the bread they got from Truth.

Jazzie gazed over at her man with a gentle smile then mumbled, "I wonder if he would be a good father?"

Chapter 6

Detective Bryant threw on his black tactical gear then loaded two magazines into his twin Glock 40's. He was half way down the steps when he realized he forgot to put on his body armor.

Detective Bryant rushed back inside, grabbed his Protech Trimax Tactical vest then fastened it to his body. He grabbed a bottle of Seagrams Gin off the living room table then took a couple swigs. The bitter taste of the gin made his face scrunched up.

"Man, this shit strong!" Detective Bryant frowned as he quickly swallowed the hard liquor.

Detective Bryant gulped down one more shot then slammed the bottle on top of the kitchen counter. He stared at the empty bottle for a second.

"I can't believe Martha wants a divorce. These young punks done cost me my marriage, my job, and my pension. I'm the fucking laughing stock of the precinct, shit, the whole city. It's time I make some niggaz feel my pain."

Detective Bryant hopped in his black '79 Pontiac Firebird and adjusted his rearview mirror. He slowly backed out of the garage, his Firebird purred like a Lion as water dripped out of the dual exhaust. As the garage door slowly closed Detective Bryant hit the gas a few times, the front end rose up each time. Suddenly his car darted down the alley like a jet, almost hitting a kid taking out the garbage.

****

The time read 8:30 P.M. on Detective Bryant's Timex watch. He hit the corner on 17th N Center searching for his adversaries. Detective Bryant coasted down the one way, behind limo tint, studying every man's face and posture trying to find any resemblance of his foes but came up empty handed. Seconds later, Truth pulled in front of his Aunt Lucille's house with Trouble and JaBar in tow. People rushed out of their houses trying see who was driving the cars outside beating out of control.

Truth, Trouble, and JaBar hopped out of their whips while they were still running then started dancing in the middle of the street with the hood rats. Aunt Lucille and Mary came outside with their sons to see what all the commotion was about. Andre and Black D ran up to Trouble and Truth. They were happy to see them.

"Hey nah, what yawl doing over hurr with yawl music blastin' like yawl crazy?" Aunt Lucille asked in her thick southern drawl.

"Y'all gone be deaf in a few years," Aunt Mary added.

"This how us young folks do it now, Tee-Tee. We love our music loud, plus the gurls love it," Trouble explained calmly.

"Well, gone reach in ya' pockets and give ya' favorite Tee-Tee some money. I need some cigarettes," Aunt Lucille begged her nephews with her hands out.

Truth reached inside his pockets and pulled out a wad of money. He peeled off twenty dollars then handed it to Lucille.

"Hurr you go Tee-Tee, buy yo'self a carton of cigarettes," Truth offered.

"Ahh bless yo' heart chile," Lucille praised Truth while patting him on the shoulder.

"Come on Trouble, I need some money from you too," Aunt Mary uttered with her hand already out, not accepting no for an answer.

Trouble exhaled as he stared up at the sky.

"Fo' what Tee-Tee?" Trouble questioned.

"The hell you mean what fo'? Cuz I'm broke, that's why," Aunt Mary shot back.

"You should've been a pimp the way you rape us for our money," Trouble replied as he burst out laughing handing Mary fifty dollars.

"What yawl lil niggaz been on over hurr?" Truth asked Andre.

"Man Cuz, I'm gone keep it gangsta with cha. We been laying niggaz down fo' ours," Andre replied as he cracked his knuckles and grinned.

Truth shook his head not liking what he just heard.

"Y'all need to stop that shit, Cuz. That ain't a real hustle," Truth informed his his lil cousin.

"The hell if it ain't! How you gone tell me my hustle ain't valid, Cuz!" Jason snapped back.

"Lil nigga, if you gone rob a nigga you suppose to buss a power move so you won't have to rob again, fuck hitting petty licks!" Truth grilled.

"Ok then Truth, since you talking shit, put us on then."Jason barked.

"Itz hot as a bitch over hurr, cuz. If I put something in you niggaz' hands them 16 deep boys gone be pissed, and you know itz gone get ugly," Truth countered.

"Man, fuck them niggaz, Truth! Them niggaz respect our Gangsta, especially after we trunked them two Detecs the other day while they were tricking off with dopefiend Pinky. We taped that shit too and sent it to the news on they bitch ass," Black D bragged.

"Damnnn! That was y'all fools?" Trouble asked, not believing what he just heard. "Jazzie told me 'bout dat shit, y'all sum bad azz lil niggaz," Truth grinned while shaking his head. "Y'all got y'all heat on y'all now? Cuz y'all embarrassed the fuck out dem cops, you know they want some get back fo' dat shit. Plus, they got suspended indefinitely without pay too," Truth cautioned.

Andre did a lil whistle. Out of nowhere niggaz popped up out of the gangway strapped with bloodshot red eyes ready to murk something.

"See big cuz, I keep plenty shooters on deck. I wish a nigga would come through here on some fuck shit. They ass gone get flatlined," Andre assured Truth with his chest poked out.

Truth was impressed with the structure his lil cuz had on his block. Right then and there he knew he was gone put them in the game.

"Say Cuz, move yo' momz out this house then we can discuss business," Truth stated.

"It might be hard cuz they been over here forever, but I'll try," Black D replied before staring back at the house.

Seconds after Black D finished his sentence, Detective Bryant hit the gas in his Firebird. As he accelerated, his tires screamed as they dug into the pavement, splattering rocks and debris in every direction. Immediately everybody drew their pistols then started firing at Detective Bryant's vehicle. It looked like the scene from the movie "Set It Off" when Queen Latifah made her last dash past the police as they Swiss cheesed her '63 Impala. Aunt Lucille and Mary hit the floor for cover. They were used to constant gunplay and knew the procedure. Gun shots rang out as shells smacked the pavement. Detective Bryant emptied his clip, wounding a few of his rivals. Truth's cousinJason caught a bullet in the leg.

"I'm hit! I'm hit!" One of the shooters cried out as he squirmed on the pavement, trying to stop the bleeding from his wound.

Trouble rushed over to his wounded cousin while the rest of Black D's goons ran to assist the other wounded soldiersJason was bleeding rapidly from the open gun wound to his leg.

"Hang in thurr Cuz, you gone be aight!" Trouble pleaded, trying to keep Jason calm.

"Damn, my leg is burning, Trouble," Jason cried.

"I know it is cuz, I'ma get you to the hospital."

Luckily the bullet didn't hit any vital organs in Jason's leg, so there was hope for him.

****

Detective Bryant's heart was beating vigorously. He hadn't planned on being on the defense. He thought he was going to be the only aggressor during his mission. Truth, JaBar, and Andre emptied their clips as they ran towards Detective Bryant's Firebird. Luckily he managed to get away. Detective Bryant said a quick prayer thanking God for reminding him to wear his vest.

Detective Bryant patted his chest, checking for any traces of fresh blood. Suddenly he felt something warm on his legs, which triggered his senses to look down. Detective Bryant instantly panicked seeing his pants were drenched in blood.

"Fuck!!! They shot me in the fuckin nuts! Fuck!!!" He yelled as panic overcame him causing him to faint.

Aunt Lucille and Mary rose from the floor slowly once the shooting ceased. They were hysterical. They immediately started screaming out their boys' names, praying they were okay.

"Jason! D! Andre! Truth! Trouble! Y'all okay?" Aunt Mary screamed. "Lord, let these boys be okay," She prayed.

After the gun battle ended, the block resembled a ghost town. Shattered glass and empty shell casing littered the broken pavement, the scent of gun powder lingered in the air, the neighborhood residents were skeptical to raise from the floor in fear of the shooting reoccurring.

"Fuck! Jason got hit, Folks!" Truth yelled while clutching his fist tightly.

"We gotta move from over hurr, I can't take no mo' of this shit!" Aunt Lucille hollered.

"Please Lord, let my baby be okay. I know he ain't no saint, but please watch over him for me," Aunt Mary moaned while looking up at the sky.

She knew their kids weren't saints, but regardless of the fact, these were their kids. She didn't see the bad in them like everybody else did, Mary loved her kids unconditionally. She knew she had to be there for her youngest son to make sure he pulled threw.

****

"We hurr now cuz, I got you lil nigga," Trouble stated, breathing heavily.

Trouble pulled up to the emergency room entrance then parked. He ran to the passenger side of his whip snatching the door open.

"Ahhhh! My leg!!" Jason screamed in agony.

"Man up cuz, we hurr now. The doctors' gone get you right," Trouble assured Jason as he dragged him out the car. "Somebody please help me! My cousin been shot! Somebody help fuckin' now!" Trouble demanded while dragging Jason inside the emergency room barely keeping his balance.

Nurses ran to their assistance, taking over the situation. Once Trouble saw that his cousin was in good hands, he quickly vanished. He been around long enough to know that the hospital would have to call the police and report the shooting. By him having an open warrant back in Louisiana, he wasn't taking any chances. He knew if they questioned him they'd run his name, and he'd get extradited. Trouble was hustling too good in Milwaukee. At this point in his life, jail was not an option.

****

Once Jason was done being treated for his wounds, two homicide detectives were on site to question him. Jason stuck to the G-Code not giving the Detectives any information. They tried to outsmart him with the good cop bad cop routine, but Jason watched enough gangster movies to know when cops were on straight bullshit. The detectives were pissed at Jason for holding out on them.

"Fine! You don't want to help us then we can't hunt the fuckers down that did this to you!" One of the detectives barked.

Loud talking could be heard in the hallway as Mary stopped in front of Jason's door. The detectives were aggressively interrogating Jason when Mary entered the room.

"Leave my son alone you ugly mutha fuckaz! If he don't know who shot him you can't force him to lie, you no good bitches!" Mary snapped.

"Ma'am, we're trying to conduct an investigation here. We can arrest you for interfering in police business!" One of the detectives stated.

"Yawl should've had your asses on patrol when the shit went down instead of sitting yawl asses outside of Dunkin' Donuts stuffing yawl face!"

Mary was heated. She stared the two detectives down with a menacing scowl, letting them know she meant business. Moments later, a female doctor entered the room advising the detectives to leave. The detective didn't leave without a fight, but they knew they would be in trouble if they didn't follow the doctor's orders. Once the situation was under control, the doctor checked Jason's vitals then studied her chart.

"How you doing, Champ?" The doctor questioned.

"Hey," Jason grumbled.

"I'm sorry you had to deal with those stupid detectives under these conditions, they have no respect for people. All they care about is getting answers. From the looks of it, you're doing well."

Jason had a blank look on his face wondering if the doctor had any bad news. The doctor turned towards Mary, explaining what was going on with her son.

"We'll be releasing him in the morning, but for now, he needs his rest. The pain medication is going to make him extremely drowsy."

Aunt Mary thanked the doctor for taking good care of her son then shook her hand. The medication was slowly taking effect on Jason. His eyes started getting heavy. He kept blinking, trying to fight his sleep but was losing the battle. Mary gazed at her son as he slowly faded away to la la land.

"Son, be strong. I'm glad God was watching over you. If he would've taken you away from me I would've committed suicide," Aunt Mary stated gently as she rubbed Jasons forehead.

"He's a warrior sis, we some strong people," Lucille uttered as she comforted Mary.

A tear slid down Jason's cheek as he stared back at his mother and Aunt.

"I'm sorry for putting y'all through this," Jason mumbled.

"Hush son, save yo' energy, get some rest nah, ya hurr," Mary whispered softly.

Seconds later Jason fell into a deep slumber.

****

The following morning Truth gave his Aunts money for rent and security deposit for a single family house on 68th N. Capitol Dr. He felt it was time for them to move out of the hood due to the conditions getting worse. Truth called his squad and told them to meet him at his car wash. Twenty minutes later the whole squad was on deck, Trouble, Boss, JaBar, Andre, and Black D.

"So what's the word on that Fire-bird, Andre?" Truth asked.

"Yo' guess is good as minez, cuz. I never saw that car in the hood before." Andre assured Truth.

"Well, keep yo' ears the streets so you don't get caught slippin' again. That was a close call," Truth ordered.

"Cuz, that shit won't ever happen again," Andre made known.

Truth walked towards his office door, making sure it was locked. After assuring that it was, he took a seat behind his desk then kicked his feet up on his desktop. Truth studied the crew's facial expressions then shook his head.

"I called yawl hurr because I'm 'bout to get a shipment in soon. I need everybody on their "A" game, Folks. Shit 'bout to get real. I'm 'bout to flood the streets with these bricks, so you niggaz 'bout to really eat. Watch these niggaz out chea, don't let no new niggaz yawl circles. You gotta keep the grass cut cuz itz plenty snakes in the grass that want yawl' spots and will do anything to knock you off. We all family hurr, we got to be on top of our business not just in it. Now Black D and Andre, I'm gone hit yawl with a split first to see how yawl do with that.

In this organization we stack our paper first before we go spending. If yawl niggaz do what yawl suppose to do I'm expecting yawl to be copping yawl own brick in no time. I ain't doing this shit forever so now is the time to stack as much bread as you can so you can continue yo' hustle once I'm done." Truth spoke with authority. Truth led the meeting like a 5 Star General while his soldiers sat quietly. "I'll give yawl a call once I'm good," Truth dictated as he rose to his feet and stared all his troops in their eyes, studying their body language.

"Man East, I sure can't wait to get back to the money, plus the weekend coming up too," Boss replied as he rubbed his hands together while smiling.

Wednesday through Saturday were the best days out of the week because they were payday for most folks. Bzzzz, Bzzzz, Bzzzz, was the sound of Truth's cell phone.

"Hello," he answered.

"Hey Truth, the plane landed," Joel stated calmly.

Truth knew that was the code for the dope being on deck. He couldn't help but to grin as dollars signs filled his eyes.

"Where can I meet you?" Joel asked.

"I got a spot on the Southside, meet me on 27th N. National," Truth relayed.

"Okay buddy, don't have me waiting too long," Joel advised.

"Don't worry I won't," Truth responded before hanging up.

Truth pulled into the Amoco gas station twenty minutes later. Joel followed him into an alley then made the exchange.

"Drive safe Truth, I'm not ready to fight for your life just yet," Joel expressed with grave concern.

"My spot not too far from hurr, shiiidd, I'm not ready for you to be fighting fo' my life yet either," Truth shot back with a slight grin.

Once Truth made it to his stash house, he quickly opened the duffle bag. The bricks had Gucci prints stamped on them, which meant the dope was A-1. Truth reached in between the sofa cushions then retrieved his Pirate Skull butterfly knife. Truth placed some old newspaper on the kitchen table then cut into the brick wrapping with precision like a doctor on the operating table.

Cocaine dust lingered through the air, once the brick was busted wide open. Truth was appalled by the way the dope sparkled like flawless VVS1 Diamonds. He was smiling from ear to ear. Truth knew in a matter of time he would see another million if he could keep a good supply of dope. He picked up his cell phone then called Joel.

"So Truth, are they pretty or what?" Joel asked while grinning.

Truth was smiling on the other side of the phone as he responded, "Ahh man, these bitches beautiful."

"I could only do ten for now, Truth. We gotta prove we can move those in a timely matter before it really start snowing."

"Shit, I'll pay you now for these bitches."

"Whoahh, that's 140 G'z, Truth," Joel coughed.

"We'll meet up tomorrow. That lil money ain't shit to me, Joel," Truth concluded.

"Okay Truth, if you insist. I'll see you tomorrow then," Joel responded.

"Good looking out too, Joel," Truth stated.

"No problem, you just promise me your not going to draw too much attention to yourself," Joel voiced seriously.

"Don't worry 'bout me, Joel, I know what to do and what not to do," Truth assured Joel.

"Okay, I'll see you tomorrow then."

The men ended the call. Truth called Mileena and asked her to come over. Once she made it to the stash house, they headed straight to the kitchen. They turned six bricks into ten bricks utilizing their whip game. Truth gave Mileena nine ounces for helping him out.

"Damn, this shit glass, Truth!" Mileena noted eagerly.

"Ain't it?" Truth responded while gazing at the mound of crack cocaine.

"Papi, you came up this time with this batch."

"It pays to know people that know people," Truth bragged.

"Don't be surprised if I be back at you, cuz they gone eat this shit right up," Mileena assured Truth.

"You know I got you too, babe," Truth promised.

Truth stacked ten bricks into a duffle bag then placed the rest in his stash spot in the basement. He called a cab to take him back to his car wash. He wasn't taking any chances riding dirty. If Truth happened to get pulled over the case would definitely be Federal, and he would be facing twenty to life easily.

The crack laws were biased towards African Americans, where as if you got caught with powder the time was drastically lesser depending on your past arrest history and what you got caught with. Before the Johnny cab arrived, Truth called his squad and told them to meet him back at the wash ASAP. Once inside the cab, Truth eye'd the driver, wondering if he could be an undercover because cops were starting to get hip to drug dealers using cabs to bust moves. Beads of sweat started to trickle down his forehead as they weaved in and out of traffic. Truth was definitely paranoid.

The cabbie noticed Truth's uneasiness as he peeped through his rear view mirror. To be extra cautious, Truth ordered the driver to drop him off a few blocks away from his car wash. As he walked down the street, Truth prayed he didn't get hounded by vice squad. After all, he did look suspect walking down the street carrying a duffle bag. Truth was a block away from his destination when suddenly he heard police siren storming towards him.

The squad car came to a screeching halt as the driver slammed on the brakes. Truth almost shitted on himself.

"Stay calm, stay calm, they probably gone pull off once they see I'm not the one they're looking for," Truth whispered under his breath.

"Did you see a man running this way wearing a red jogging suit?" Asked the officer behind the wheel.

Truth's heart was beating so fast his body temperature rose fifteen degrees as his deodorant turned into beads of sweat, dripping like water, down his arm pits.

"No Sir, I ain't seen nobody that fit that description," Truth stated nervously.

"Thanks man. If you don't mind me asking, why you carrying a duffle bag? Ain't no guns in there, young fella?" The officer asked with one eyebrow arched.

"I'm 'bout to go to my aunt house and do a lil laundry," Truth lied, not knowing if he should break out and run.

Pssh, Psshh, "We have a black male shot on 13th N. Locust, all units in the area please respond." The dispatcher blared over the squad car radio.

"Take care son, sorry we bothered you." The officer apologized as he gunned his squad car towards the crime scene.

Truth took a deep breath as the squad car sped off. His stomach started bubbling as he walked towards the car wash, he couldn't wait to sit on the toilet.

****

Truth stepped out of the bathroom feeling ten pounds lighter.

"Man, that was a close call. Thank you Lord for letting me slide this time."

Once everybody was on deck at the wash, Truth locked the front entrance then escorted his team back to his office.

"Boss, here's six bricks for you, and two for you Trouble. Think you can handle it, cuz?" Truth asked seriously.

"Huh bruh, this is a lot of dope, but I'm ready to step up to the plate," Trouble shot back confidently.

"Andre and Black D, here's a split, I'd advise y'all to bust this all the way down. Y'all should at least see five G'z off it easy. All I want back is $2,000. Remember, y'all gotta invest in this shit cuz that front shit is punk shit," Truth stressed.

"Gotcha cuz, we gone come up off this here." Black D noted.

"Well thatz it, y'all niggaz make sho' you drive with caution, don't be bumpin' yawl music all loud and shit. Fuck it, throw y'all seat belts on too," Truth commanded.

"Damn nigga, you too noid," Trouble joked.

"Nigga, you suppose to be, it ain't sweet out here. Itz betta to be safe than sorry," Boss added.

"Real talk Boss, real talk bruh," Truth stated as he gave Boss some dap.

****

Future was putting the finishing touches on a track he was working on for his mixtape. He had been busy trying to get his features from artists and sending tracks to producers. Future developed a relationship with the strippers around Atlanta. He started making songs for them to dance to and was slowly making a name for himself. Future decided to call his homegirl Honey. He had a surprise for her.

"Hey Honey," he spoke into the phone.

"Whatz good Future?" Honey replied excitedly.

"I made a song for you," he stated.

"Wow, is it hot?" Honey questioned.

"Come on now Honey, you know how I get down," Future shot back confidently.

"If itz hot and I make a lot of money tonight, I'm gone give you a private dance when the club closes," Honey teased.

"Well get ready to party then shawty," Future assured Honey.

Honey started smiling as she twirled her fingers threw her hair.

"I guess I'll see you in a few," she flirted back.

"Fo sho," Future spoke.

As they hung up from one another, smiles crept across their faces. Honey was definitely feeling Future. He had to make another call to his homie, MC Breed.

"Hello," MC Breed answered.

"Whuzz good Breed, you coming out tonight?" He asked.

"Where you tryna go?" MC Breed questioned.

"To Club 112, I got a song I wanna break to see how the crowd react." Future explained.

"I'll roll, especially to see some big booty's clap," Breed joked, truthfully.

"Well, I'll reserve you a table in V.I.P. What you drinking on?"

Future made a mental note of the drink request.

"Remy Martin and get me a bottle of Moet too. I hope you put a few tracks aside for me too, bruh." Breed requested.

"I gotcha pimpin', you know you in with me." Future uttered before ending the call. Bzzz, Bzzz, Bzzzz, "Who calling me now?" Future wondered as he flipped his cell phone open. "Hello," he answered.

"Whuzz zatnin bruh?" Truth spoke to his brother.

"Man bruh, I ain't heard from you in a minute!" Future responded excitedly.

"Bruh, all type of shit been goin' on, but I'm good." Truth reported.

"Huh bruh, you need to move down here, the Mill gone kill yo' ass," Future shot back.

"Don't worry 'bout me, bruh, I got this hurr. Fuck all dat shit, you know my birthday coming up, and I'm throwing a party in Miami. I got a mansion too." Truth boasted excitedly.

"Huh bruh."

"So bring all the strippers you know from the clubs with you and some of yo' celebrity friends too."

"You know I'm gone come through for you, bruh."

"I been seriously thinking 'bout fuckin' with the rap game, Bruh. I hope you ready when I come with dat money," Truth expressed.

"Bruh, you know I'm riding with you, but you gotta lay yo' guns down if you wanna hop into this game cuz the Fedz will be all up in our shit, and I don't want to blow up, then turn around and get indicted," Future made clear.

Truth shook his head thinking his brother was being too paranoid.

"I feel you mane, I'ma get out before hand." Truth explained.

"Act like it," Future shot back as he began to smile.

"Oh, I was calling to tell you Jason got shot in a drive by, but he was just grazed on the leg."

Future shook his head as he clutched his fist tightly.

"Bruh, promise me once you reach yo' mark you gone walk away. You all I got left, bruh," Future uttered with grave concern as a tear dripped from his eye.

"I promise you I am, bruh, and we gone be the next Death Row," Truth assured Future.

"Aight bruh. Did you get them niggaz that did that shit to Jason?" Future asked as he wiped away his tears.

"We aired 17th straight the fuck out, bruh. If that mudda fucka alive he gotta have nine lives."

"Ok then, thatz all I'm talking 'bout, what else is up?"

"Shit mane, Trouble getting his weight up, Dre and Black D on my team now. Oh, I moved Aunt Lucille and Mary out the hood, they on 68th N. Capitol now."

"Cool, cool, that's good. I'm down here bangin' out these tracks and pluggin' strippers with personalized songs, and they lovin' it."

"Yo time gone come bruh, keep grindin', we gotta make something happen so momz could be proud of us up in Heaven."

"Man, I miss her Truth."

"I do too bruh." The brothers fell silent for a few seconds as they reminisced about the good times with their mother. "FYI, the party gone be an all white party too, bruh," Truth stated, breaking the silence.

"Okay mane, I'm gone act a ass too boy!" Future stated with excitement.

"I'm already knowing. You need anything?" Truth questioned.

"I can use a few G'z to buy some more equipment." Future explained.

"Gotcha bruh. Well, I'ma holla at cha later, see you at the party, bruh," Truth expressed.

"Love ya bruh," Future replied.

"Love ya too." Truth stated as he ended the call.

Chapter 7

Heaven tossed and turned in her Queen sized bed for hours, as her body yearned for Truth. She placed a pillow between her legs as she dreamed of her love.

"You like that, baby?" Truth whispered gingerly.

"Yes! Yes!" Heaven moaned as Truth's tongue gently slid over her throbbing clitoris.

She envisioned them alone on Bradford beach, naked, engaging in sensual sex, while rain drops trickled from the skies over their tangled bodies.

Juices flowed from Heaven's womb, soaking the pillow. She slowly arched her back, positioning Truth's head in between her slippery thighs, grinding his face while the tidal waves splashed in the background. Heaven was approaching her climax when suddenly her cat leaped onto her bed, bringing her back to reality.

"Domino, what is your problem! Damn, that dream felt real, bad cat," Heaven pouted as she scolded her cat.

Heaven couldn't understand why Truth was with Jazzie. She felt he deserved someone better. She had her life together, she owned her house, her credit score was 770, and didn't have any kids. If she wanted to she could very well have any professional man she wanted, but she was attracted to a D-Boy.

Heaven was raised in a household with both parents. Her parents got married after they graduated High School. Her father went on to become a dermatologist, while her mother became a civil lawyer. Heaven promised her parents she would finish her schooling first then start a career before having kids.

Heaven started massaging her cat's neck. Domino was enjoying the affection he was getting. He stretched his body out then started purring. Heaven sat Domino on the bed then got up to fix a glass of water. She reached inside the cupboard for her favorite cup and poured a glass of cold water. The cold water was refreshing, quenching her thirst. Heaven placed her cup on the counter top and stared at a flyer that was left on her car windshield. Heaven studied the flyer as she placed it back on her kitchen table.

"I definitely will be showing my face at Truth's birthday bash, plus it's in Miami. I need a vacation anyway, so this will be the perfect reason to take one. I'm gone have to run to Chicago to go shopping. I gotta make sure nobody wearing what I'm wearing. I'm tryna turn heads when I show up and have Truth's nose all up my ass," Heaven stated as she strolled back to her bedroom.

Heaven turned on her T.V., popped in a porno tape, pulled out her vibrator then finished herself off since her cat interrupted her erotic dream. After satisfying her sexual appetite, she was sound asleep with a kool-aid smile on her face. Truth was still on her mind. Heaven knew deep in her heart someday she would have him all to herself.

****

Bzzzz Bzzzzz Bzzzz Bzzzzz was the sound of Truth's cell phone. He was in a deep slumber. Jazzie purposely wore him out so he wouldn't have any energy to run the streets all night, she hated sleeping alone.

"Damn baby, answer yo' phone," Jazzie mumbled groggily.

Truth didn't respond so Jazzie took it upon herself to answer his phone.

"Hello," Jazzie whispered. Heaven's heart skipped a beat. She didn't expect Jazzie to answer. "Hello," Jazzie repeated, this time with an attitude.

Heaven thought about saying something slick to piss Jazzie off but figured it would be childish of her, so she simply hung up.

"I wonder who that was?" Jazzie wondered while staring at Truth. "It's too late to be arguing, I'll bring this up to him in the morning."

Being that she was exhausted, Jazzie flopped back on the bed and fell back asleep.

****

Thick weed smoke floated throughout Truth's living room as he ran bill after bill through his money counting machine. His bill for the cocaine Joel fronted him was $140,000. Once he had it counted up, he wrapped the money in thousand dollar rubberbands. Truth picked up his burn out cell phone then called Joel. He picked up on the third ring.

"Hello," Joel sang into the phone.

"Joel, I'm ready fo' ya, come pick yo' scratch up," Truth responded.

"Where you at?" Joel asked as he scratched his hands.

"At home," Truth replied.

"Okay, I'm on my way to the office. I'll pick it up along the way. If you can put the money inside a brief case, I'd appreciate it," Joel requested.

"I don't own a briefcase, mane. Maybe you can bring a empty one," Truth responded.

"I can do that. See you in thirty minutes then," Joel confirmed.

"Aight." Just as Truth pressed "end" on his cell phone, his stomach started to growl. "I'm hungry as a mudda fucka. Jazzie 'bout to fix me some breakfast," Truth mumbled to himself. "Jazzie!" He screamed into the next room.

"What!" Jazzie yelled back.

"I'm hungry, won't you make me some grits, eggs, and sausages!" He ordered.

"I ain't no damn maid," Jazzie whispered as a frown formed on her face.

She was still pissed about the call Truth got in the middle of the night.

"You hurr me woman! Fix me some damn breakfast!" Truth commanded.

Jazzie rolled her eyes as she built up enough courage to stand up to Truth, "I ain't yo' maid, nigga!"

He did a double take as he bit down on his bottom lip.

"Da fuck you just say, Jazz?" Truth rose from his chair and whispered, "Who dis bitch think she talkin' to like dat?" Truth mumbled.

"You heard me nigga!" Jazzie yelled back.

"Tha last time I checked, I thought I paid all the bills round hurr. I take care of yo' lazy ass! So get up and cook a nigga some breakfast fo' yo' ass be wearing some Great America glasses 'round dis bitch!"

Jazzie ignored Truth. She started flipping through a magazine while tapping her feet on the floor frantically.

"Who da fuck you got calling yo' phone private at 1:35AM! Huh nigga?" Jazzie barked at Truth.

"Bitch, don't question me like you standing on something. Bitch, I'll smash yo' shit in!" Truth snapped back, clinching his teeth.

"Who tha fuck was it, Truth! I don't give a fuck if you hit me! I ain't scared of you!" Jazzie cried, trying to call Truth's bluff.

His blood began to boil as he slowly walked towards Jazzie and snatched her by the throat.

"If the number showed up private how da fuck I know who called, silly bitch? Huh?" Truth whispered, verbally assaulting her.

Jazzie started gagging as tears slid down her face. Truth applied more pressure around Jazzie's throat, causing her eyes to buck. Jazzie started feeling weak as Truth held a firm grip around her neck.

Bzzzz Bzzzz Bzzzz Bzzzz was the sound of Truth's cell phone vibrating as it fell off the table, breaking him out of his menacing rage. Truth loosened his grip and Jazzie dropped to the floor gasping for air. He kneeled down and grabbed his cell phone.

"Hello!" Truth answered.

"Whoah, this me, I'm in the lobby," Joel stated.

"My fault Joel, I'll buzz you up," Truth replied as he gazed over at Jazzie lying on the floor looking a hot mess.

He kneeled down then kissed Jazzie on the forehead.

"I know that was a bitch that called, Truth. Let me find out who she is, I'ma kill her," Jazzie threatened.

Truth stared at Jazzie for a brief moment, exhaled deeply then shook his head.

"Get yo' ass up and fix my breakfast like I said with yo' stank ass." The doorbell rang, taking Truth's attention off of Jazzie. "Who is it?" He yelled.

"Santa Clause! Nah, it's me Joel!"

"Fix yo' self up Jazzie, I got company," Truth uttered aggressively.

Jazzie mean mugged Truth as she rose off the floor. Truth opened the door then greeted Joel with a light hug. He led Joel into the living room to do the money exchange. Joel grinned when he saw the mound of money sitting on the table.

"What you wearing today, Joel?" Truth questioned.

"This Armani, you like?" Joel replied as he rubbed his chest.

"I'm diggin' it, mane. Hurr's tha money, just ran it through the money counter, it's all there."

Joel popped the locks on his briefcase then neatly placed the stacks of money inside. Jazzie stepped out of the bathroom after fixing herself up.

"Hi Jazzie!" Joel politely stated, not knowing Jazzie just had the life choked out of her.

"Oh hey Joel, you staying for breakfast?" She inquired.

"I'm sorry, I can't this time, Jazzie. I'm in a rush," he admitted.

"I understand," Jazzie hinted as she rolled her eyes at Truth.

Joel was ready to leave once he had all of his money.

"Nice doing business with you, Truth. You know when you'll be ready for another batch?" Joel asked.

"I'll let you know so answer yo' phone," Truth uttered in a joking manner.

"Okay then, let me get out of here. I'm due in court at 9:30AM," Joel said and checked the table again, making sure he didn't leave anything behind.

"Handle that then." Truth expressed.

The men exchanged handshakes as Truth escorted Joel to the door. As the door shut Truth wondered what had gotten into Jazzie, she never came at him sideways. He flopped down in his favorite chair, then flipped through a DuPont Registry Magazine. While flipping through each page, Truth pictured himself inside the foreign whips.

Truth licked his finger before flipping the next page. His eyes bucked when he saw the candy red Dodge Viper, he instantly fell in love.

"Jazzie! Come hurr! Check this out!" Truth called out excitedly.

Jazzie strolled into the living room with much attitude then placed her hand on her hip.

"What?" She replied nonchantly as she handed Truth his breakfast.

"Check this Dodge Viper out. Can you picture me rollin' this?"

Jazzie glanced at the picture inside the DuPont Registry Magazine. Immediately her pussy got wet.

"Damn baby, I love this car, what color would you get?" Her anger disappeared as she stared at the car.

"Umm, black or blue, maybe even white." Truth replied.

"You gone bust niggaz heads with this one here, bae." Jazzie concluded as she handed Truth the magazine back.

Just that fast Jazzie forgot about the fight she had with Truth moments ago. She loved when Truth spent money because she knew she was getting something too. So she chalked the fight up and concentrated on buttering Truth up.

"I wouldn't bring it back hurr though, I'd leave the Viper in Atlanta so I can blend in with the ballers thurr," Truth professed.

"That's smart thinking, baby. These niggaz wouldn't understand it if you came through stunting in this mutha fucka, I can picture the look on they face too." Jazzie stated, building Truth up.

Truth envisioned himself behind the wheel of the Dodge Viper sliding threw the hood. Bad as I wanna stunt on these fuck boys, that's all they'll need to see to go running they mouth to the Feds, he thought to himself. Truth's cell phone danced on the dining room table.

"Hand me my phone, Jaz." Truth instructed.

"Here you go, Daddy."

Jazzie handed Truth his cell phone, then stuck her hand inside Truth boxers massaging his snake. She pulled his boxers down low enough so she could pull his snake out then placed it inside her hot mouth.

"Whuz zatnin?" Truth greeted into the phone.

"Cuz, we need another split." Andre replied.

"You got all tha bread?" Truth asked.

"Yea cuz," Andre confirmed.

"Okay, I'm gone put something real nice together for y'all. Let me get dressed cuz, and I'll ride down on y'all." Truth promised.

"Don't be all day cuz, it's boomin' over here." Andre explained.

"Matter of fact, call Trouble, I forgot he was holding a extra thang." Truth replied.

"Well, let fam know I'm comin', you know he be bustin' all his shit down." Andre requested.

"Aight cuz, I gotcha." Truth concluded.

Truth dropped his cell phone then closed his eyes as Jazzie worked her tongue up and down on his swollen shaft. It didn't take long for Truth to reach his climax and release his sweet nectar inside Jazzie's mouth. He jumped in the shower after his morning dose of head. He through on a Gucci linen short set with the matching Gucci print Dukey's and a Gucci sun visor, he was dopeboy fresh.

"I'ma holla at cha later, Jaz. I'm heading to the storage to get my old school and get a oil change." Truth explained.

"Aight baby. Oh wait, I need some money so I can go shopping."

Truth dug into his pocket and tossed Jazzie a stack.

"Don't spend it all in one place." He instructed.

"Oh, I won't." Jazzie replied with a big smile.

She danced to the bathroom like a happy kid then slammed the door. Jazzie had just told Truth a lie. She actually had different plans for the money that could jeopardize everything she had going.

****

Heaven was on her way back to her office when suddenly her "check engine" light popped on.

"Fuck! I hope this ain't nothing major, it's always something," Heaven complained.

She decided to stop by Jiffy Lube on 70th N. Capital Dr. to get a diagnostic test. A few cars were ahead of Heaven, so she sat patiently 'til a stall was open. Heaven checked her rearview when she heard the thunderous bass coming from afar. The bass started to get louder and louder. Heaven wondered if it was a car or truck coming her way. To her surprise, it was Truth behind her in his 1975 cocaine white Chevy Caprice convertible on triple gold Dayton's and Vogues Tires. Heaven was excited, but she played it off pretending she didn't know Truth was in line behind her.

Truth was so into his music he didn't notice the car in front of him. He was banging Tupac's "The Game's Been Good to Me" while puffing on a blunt. Heaven pulled her truck inside the garage slowly as the mechanic guided her in.

"How can I help you ma'am?" The Jiffy Lube mechanic inquired.

"My check engine light is on. Can you do a diagnostic test for me? I hope this ain't nothing major," Heaven stated as she brushed the hair out of her face.

"No problem, turn the car off for me," the mechanic instructed as he wiped his greasy hands with a clean rag.

Heaven slowly stepped out of her vehicle. Truth was surprised to see her. He started honking his horn, trying to catch Heavan attention. Truth hit his horn twice, Bumm! Bumm!

"Heaven! Come hurr gurl!" Truth yelled, summoning her towards his whip.

Heaven swung her head back, rolled her eyes, then grinned.

"I ain't a girl, I'm a grown ass woman," Heaven shot back sarcastically.

Truth's neck stiffened up after hearing Heaven's smart response. As Heaven strutted towards Truth, her Chanel Stiletto's echoed as she took each step. She leaned on Truth's door then tapped him on his chest.

"You following me now?" Heaven asked seductively.

Truth looked Heaven up and down as he licked his dry lips.

"I guess I am. You looking good in that skirt, gurl," Truth complimented Heaven while grinning.

"Thanks, you not half stepping in yo' Gucci fit," Heaven shot back.

"No wonder the sun shining so bright, look at that million dollar smile yo' fine ass flashing," Truth flirted back as he grabbed Heaven's hand and massaged it.

"Nah, the sun out because you stepped out the house smiling with that gold grill of yours," Heaven shot back.

"How you been sweetie?" Truth asked.

"I've been swamped with work," Heaven replied as she brushed her hair to the side.

"Damn, all work and no play Shawty?" Truth teased.

"I play Truth, just on my terms," she replied.

"Oh okay, Ms. Independent," Truth stated sarcastically.

"You damn right," Heaven replied.

"When you gone let me taste all this?" Truth insinuated while pointing at Heaven's body.

"Hmmphh, when you get rid of yo' wife," Heaven fumed with attitude.

"My wife?" Truth smiled.

"Did I stutter? Yeah yo' wife, letting the bitch answer the phone and shit," Heaven hissed while rolling her eyes.

"So that was you that called last night restricted?" Truth clarified as he nodded his head and grinned.

"Maybe it was, maybe it wasn't, you not dumb." Heaven confessed while looking away.

"Probably was yo' ass," Truth laughed.

"You'll never find out," Heaven smirked as she poked Truth in the chest and gave him a wink.

Truth stepped out of his car and poked Heaven back. A poke fight ensued afterwards. They played like High School sweethearts. Without any warning, Truth pulled Heaven close to his body. Her heart skipped a beat as the pleasant scent of Gucci cologne lingered into her nostrils. Suddenly they locked eyes for at least ten seconds. There was a moment of silence until the mechanic walked up.

"Ma'am, your car is gone need an oil change."

Heaven wiped her forehead then sighed, "Whoah, I, I, I gotta go, Truth."

"I guess I'll see you around," Truth replied.

"Yup, at yo' birthday party," Heaven whispered as she walked away.

****

Jazzie spread her arms as the Correctional Officer ran the metal detector over her body.

"Ma'am, you're gonna have to take your belt off and place it in your locker," the Correctional Officer instructed.

"Aight, are you done?" Jazzie complained with her nose turnt up.

The overweight Correctional Officer mugged her as he shook his head.

"Almost, we have to check your I.D to make sure this is you," the guard explained.

"Damn, I ain't under arrest," Jazzie shot back.

"Sorry Ma'am, this is prison procedure." He apologized.

This was Jazzie's first visit to a prison, and Federal at that. Law was staffed at Oxford Federal Penitentiary. Now that he had Jazzie on his turf he knew he had to lay his pimping down to keep her around. The Unit Sgt. called Law's name over the intercom, letting him know he had a visit. Law was engaged in a heated game of spades. He stood up then slapped his hand on the table.

"Y'all can fight over this lil money, a pimp got places to go, people to see." He joked.

Law rushed back to his room to get fresh. He quickly changed into his pressed jeans and polo shirt then sat down on his bunk. He threw on a pair of blue gators to compliment his outfit, Law wanted Jazzie to know even though he was in prison he was still living good. He managed to get some Muslim prayer oil from a fellow convict, so he put a lil dab on his hand then rubbed it over his neck and shirt.

Law had to go to the men's room to check his appearance and take a leak. He washed his hands with the pink liquid soap from the dispenser then gazed into the mirror. Yusef was about to go on a visit too, so he was in the mirror checking himself as well.

"You going on tha corner too, Law?" Yusef asked as he wiped his face.

"Yup, my bottom bitch finally made her way up," Law replied.

"Shiidd, we might as well mob up there together," the fellow inmate stated.

"I ain't trippin' bruh." Law stated.

As they walked towards the visiting room, Law and Yusef made small talk seeing that they weren't friends.

"Strip convicts! Y'all know the drill," a tall white officer commanded coldly.

Law and Yusef stared at each other, shook their heads then proceeded to strip their clothes off slowly.

"Come on Wilson, why you strip searching us goin' to the visit?" Law asked.

"Cuz I can! I didn't sentence you, the judge did. Now strip or I'll terminate your visits! Hurry up! Turn around! Spread yo' cheeks! Okay! Hand me your shoes!" The correction officer instructed.

The C.O. rubbed his dick as he gave orders. He envisioned himself sodomizing one of the men. The C.O. knew in the free world he couldn't make a black man do nothing, so he would abuse his power while at work.

"This some bullshit," Yusef mumbled.

As the two men got dressed they didn't say a word, getting stripped searched was demeaning enough. The guards tried their best to strip the inmates of their dignity. As the men entered the visiting room, Yusef's kids came storming towards him, giving him a big hug. Law strutted over to Jazzie like he was on the hoe stroll. Jazzie greeted Law with a big bear hug. She tried to kiss him, but he turned his face.

"Bitch, hold tha fuck up, how you gone try to kiss a pimp? I don't know where yo' lips been," Law stated coldly.

"So that's how you treat a bitch, huh?" Jazzie whined with a sad face.

"I may be in jail, but itz still pimpin', bitch," Law made known as he took a seat and crossed his legs.

"I see you ain't changed a bit," Jazzie replied, smiling ear to ear.

"You miss a pimp, huh?" Law stated while rubbing his nostrils.

"Something like that," Jazzie responded happily.

"Yo' nigga know where you at?" He questioned.

"Nope, fuck him, he choked me out this morning over some bullshit," Jazzie's head sank in her chair from the embarrassment.

"I don't see no bruises on you, bitch."

"Look at my neck."

"Dayuuum, da fuck you do?"

"He got mad cuz I confronted him 'bout somebody calling his phone restricted at one in da morning," Jazzie explained.

She was trying her best to get Law to feel sorry for her so he wouldn't bring up the fact that she broke bad on him. Law studied Jazzie face. He could spot a bullshit story from a mile away.

"So you answered the nigga phone?"

"Hell yeah! I can't wait 'til you get out, Daddy."

"If I fuck back with you, you gotta pay a fee fo' absconding, bitch."

"I know Daddy."

"I may be home sooner than you expect if I can get back in court on appeal. I got some real valuable info on a dirty cop," Law bragged with a cocky grin on his face.

Yusef was chasing his son through the visiting room. He caught him in front of Law's table.

"Sorry yawl," Yusef apologized as he yanked his son's arm.

He mumbled something to his son, letting him know he didn't approve of him acting up. Yusef did a double take when he saw Jazzie.

"Hey Jazzie," he stated with a grin.

"Oh, h-h-hey Yusef," Jazzie stuttered as her stomach dropped to the ground.

Law stared at Yusef then back at Jazzie confused.

"Yawl know each other?" Law questioned.

"He from the hood, Law," Jazzie lied.

Yusef peeped her uneasiness, and he found the predicament amusing.

"Yeah Law, we know each other from the hood."

Law's face frowned up. He didn't know if he should believe them or not. Yusef excused himself from Law's table then strutted back to his table thinking, This bitch bogus as fuck, wait til I tell Boss this shit. Yusef was Boss's right hand man before he got knocked. He was set up for a brick of crack cocaine and received fifteen years. Luckily, he didn't have any priors or he would have been facing a life bid. Jazzie and Law continued on with their visit. Jazzie couldn't believe one of Truth's soldiers caught her red handed visiting another man.

"Law, would you please excuse me? I have to go to the ladies room." Jazzie stated; she was fuming inside.

"Don't be all damn day, we only got a hour left up here."

"Okay."

Jazzie rushed off to the ladies room as the convicts did double take after double take amazed at Jazzie's beauty and luscious body. One guy got slapped by his girl for sneaking a peak at Jazzie's ass.

Jazzie paced back and forth inside the ladies room then punched the wall.

"I can't believe this shit! What are the odds of me running into Yusef! I'm busted! I wonder if he gone drop the dime? Damn!" Jazzie cried.

She splashed some water on her face then stared into the mirror. A white lady stepped through the door noticing Jazzie looking distraught.

"You okay?" The woman asked.

"Yup, just a lil tired," Jazzie replied with a fake smile.

The white lady washed her hands, gazed back at Jazzie then exited the ladies room. Jazzie tried to justify visiting Law by lying to herself.

"Truth cheating on me anyway, bitches calling and hanging up in the wee hours. Damn, I'm so confused. Who do I really want to be with? Fuck it, I'll stay with Truth 'til Law comes home." Jazzie concluded while wiping her hands with a piece of paper towel then gathered herself.

"Okay, you're a big girl, you can handle this," Jazzie told herself as she exited the restroom.

Yusef was standing at the vending machine with his son as Jazzie slowly approached. Yusef stared at Jazzie then shook his head in disgust.

"How you gone creep up here on Folks?" He quickly questioned.

Jazzie ignored Yusef. She walked by with her head to the ground, trying to conceal the embarrassment she felt deep inside. For the rest of the visit Jazzie and Law discussed their future plans.

For that moment Jazzie felt secure. The visit was coming to an end. Jazzie knew she would have to face reality soon.

"Times up Mr. Mcaffee," shouted the fat C.O.

Jazzie and Law rose from their seats and quickly embraced each other.

"Damn, I don't wanna go," Jazzie whined.

"Don't worry Jazzie, Daddy will be home soon," Law assured her.

"Hurry up then, I need you out here," Jazzie stated as she gazed into Law's eyes.

The trip back to Milwaukee seemed like an eternity. All types of thoughts crossed Jazzie's mind. She knew she crossed the line by visiting Law, but at this point there was no turning back. Tears slid down Jazzie chocolate cheeks as she began to think. How did I get caught slippin? I should've checked to see where Yusef was doing time at, damn. I'm a seasoned hoe. I wasn't supposed to get so wrapped up with Truth. This was supposed to be a temporary fling, she thought.

Jazzie exhaled deeply as she popped in Mary J Blige's "My Life" CD then skipped to her favorite song, "I'm Going Down". Mary J Blige's soulful voice blessed her ears as tears started to muster up inside her. Jazzie was a confused and a lost soul at this point. She thought she loved Truth, but after seeing Law, all her old feelings resurrected, causing her to become disoriented.

Jazzie said a prayer, "Please, don't let Truth find out I went to see Law. God, I promise if you help me I won't do it again, I swear."

Jazzie was in deep thought when her cell phone started vibrating.

"Should I answer this?" She pondered.

"Damn bitch, answer the phone," Truth mumbled on the other end.

Jazzie played it safe by not picking up because she was at least four hours away from Milwaukee, and if Truth asked where she was, she wouldn't have a good enough lie.

Truth hung up then headed to his car wash to get his car detailed. He loved his '75 Caprice. Out of all the old school cars in Milwaukee, his was one of the top in its class beside Lionel, who was a beast with his whips. As Truth cruised through the city he honked his horn, then chunked the deuces at the d boyz and hustlaz. Truth slowly approached the lights on 35th and North Avenue when Lionel pulled up on him in his two-door candy red deuce and a quarter bangin' 2pac's, "Shed so Many Tears."

They stared each other down. Lionel revved his engine a few times then grinned at Truth. Truth nodded his head then revved his engine.

"You ain't ready, my nigga!" Lionel warned Truth.

"Shiiidd bruh, my shit's not too, my nigga!" Truth shot back.

"Letz race to Sherman then!" Lionel stated as he revved his engine causing his glass packs to roar.

"Shiidd, act like it then, nigga," Truth replied as he gripped his steering wheel tightly.

Instantly the light turned green. All that could be heard was the sounds of tires screeching as they dug into the black pavement while the heavy bass rumbled from their trunks. Lionel got Truth from the take off. As they sped up North Avenue, people were pulling over trying to avoid getting rear ended. Seconds later Truth and Lionel were nose to nose, Lionel took one look at Truth then grinned.

They were quickly approaching Sherman Blvd, where there was heavy traffic. Truth thought he had the race won 'til Lionel hit his nitrous button.

"Can't fuck in my bidness!!!" Lionel yelled as his whip darted off.

Lionel couldn't stop when he reached the lights on Sherman Blvd. His heart was pounding rapidly as he approached the intersection honking his horn frantically. The lights were red, unfortunately there was no way Lionel could break his speed down in a matter of seconds. So he blew through the red light, praying to God he didn't crash into anybody.

While Truth sat at the lights he thought to himself, One day I'ma beat his ass. When the light turned green he rushed over to Lionel. He was parked on 46th N North Ave. Truth pulled up behind Lionel, hopped out and shook his hand.

"Next time I race yo' ass, I'ma put up a brick," Truth joked.

"All you gotta do is act like it, Truth. I'm trained to go," Lionel stated while rubbing his hands.

"What da fuck you got under thurr, mane?" Truth asked.

"If I tell you I'm gone have to kill you," Lionel joked.

Truth shrugged his shoulders as his eyebrows rose.

"Just curious bruh," Truth replied.

"I'll tell you one day," Lionel assured Truth as he tapped the hood of his car.

"You coming to my all white party in Miami?" Truth asked.

"You know I'ma be there, Truth. How could I miss it?" Lionel expressed.

"Itz gone be off the chain too bruh," Truth made known, then looked at his Cartier watch.

"Let me get out of hurr, Bruh, I'll holla at cha later."

Truth turned away and took a step.

"Hold up Truth, how much you letting yo' bricks go fo'?" Lionel questioned.

"Holla at Boss, he'll plug you. I'm keepin' my hands clean, Folks."

Lionel nodded his head in agreement.

"Okay, I feel ya Folks, I'll get up with Boss, just let him know you talked to me first," Lionel uttered.

"Consider it done." Truth concluded.

****

Truth pulled up to his car wash and blew his horn. One of his workers rushed over to his car to see what he wanted.

"Pull my shit in and give it the deluxe wash and spray some new car scent in it," he instructed.

"Gotcha Boss," Truth's employee muttered.

Truth took a look around his establishment then grinned when he spotted Fella, Culpepper, Milwaukee Johnny, and Gig. Truth walked towards the d-boys then locked it up with them throwing up the forks.

"Whuz zatnin yawl?" Truth greeted the gangstaz.

"Shiiidd, tryna eat like you," Milwaukee Johnny replied.

"Shiiiidd, you already eating, look at that belly, Folks," Truth shot back as everybody burst out laughing.

Moments later, a crack head strolled into the car wash.

"Who wanna buy some '96 tags fo' they car?" The crack head asked.

"Man, get yo' dirty ass up outta here with that shit," Fella grumbled.

"How 'bout a wig fo' yo' girl. I got red, black, and blonde."

Truth stared at Milwaukee Johnny, and without hesitation they all burst out laughing. They couldn't believe the nerve of this dope fiend. They were laughing so hard they were hunched down clutching their stomachs.

"How 'bout if I sang, "I Got A Pocket Full Of Stones"? The crack head suggested as he swayed from side to side.

"Act like it bitch," Truth replied.

"I gotta pocket full of stonessss, I smoked them now they all goneeeeee …"

Before the crack head could continue, everybody burst out laughing again.

"Man where ya'll find this clown ass nigga!" Gig asked.

"Since y'all laughing at my expense, won't y'all lousy mutha fuckaz at least give a nigga fiddy cent a piece so I can get some single cigarettes and a dolla worth of hog head cheese," the fiend requested.

"Shiiiidd, this ain't Red Cross nigga," Culpepper made known as he gave Fella some dap.

"Hurr ten dolllars bruh, make sure you get something to eat too," Truth instructed as he stared at the crack head wondering what type of nigga he was before he got strung out.

Truth had a soft spot for homeless people that tried to get they hustle on.

"Truth, you always saving a muhfucka," Fella joked.

"Bruh, you never know when you gone be down and out and need a blessing. I just think some good gone come out of it, thatz just the way I look at shit, bruh. " Truth replied.

"Okay then nigga, since you in the giving mood, what you gone tax me fo' three bricks?" Fella pleaded.

"I really want twenty-six cooked, but I'll take twenty-four piece, bruh."

Fella's eyes lit up.

"Bet!"

"When you want dem?" Truth asked.

"Asap, I got the money in the trunk of the Lac now," Fella stated.

"Grab it and meet me in my office."

Fella rushed out to his car and returned with a camouflage duffle bag. Truth ran the stacks of money through his money counter, making sure it was all there.

"Okay Fel, give me 'bout an hour and meet me back hurr by yo'self," Truth instructed.

"Aight Fam, I hope its that fish scale Boss been having," Fella insisted as he licked his cracked lips.

"Oh it is, I only fucks with the best," Truth assured him. "This shit jumping back as soon as the cold water hit the Pyrex, bruh." Truth boasted.

What Fella didn't know was the dope was across the street at a corner store Truth owned on the low. Nobody knew he owned it because he hired Arabs to run it to throw people off. He kept a shooter on deck at the store just in case a fool thought it was sweet to rob the store. Truth didn't know he just undercut Boss by dealing with Fella directly. Fella was trying to save a few dollars by dealing with Truth direct so he could pocket more off the middle man deal.

****

"Damn Truth, this shit glass!" Fella stated excitedly.

"You know I keeps that butta, Folks," Truth joked.

"Well, let me get outta here. I got niggaz waiting on me, I wanna catch a quick sale," Fella replied.

"Aight bruh, I ain't tryna hold you up from getting yo' money." Truth didn't know that Fella, Culpepper, and Milwaukee Johnny all went in on the bricks nor did he care. Once the dope left his hands, he didn't have a care where it went. Truth's phone started vibrating on his hip.

He flipped it open then started talking, "Whuzz zatnin?"

"What up my man," King Mitch replied.

"How you feelin' King Mitch?" Truth inquired.

"Like new money," Mitch replied.

"I see, I see, huh bruh."

The men continued to discuss plans for the bash.

"Say Truth, I got a surprise fo' yo' ass for yo' birthday," Mitch revealed.

"Word?"

Truth's head swayed to the side as he wondered what King Mitch's surprise was.

"Just make sure you got a black girl for me at the party, you know I love black pussy," King Mitch expressed with a light chuckle.

"I got you. I like surprises too, bruh. Oh, don't try to out shine me at my own party, mane," Truth specified as he began to smile.

Truth called Trouble.

"Whuz zatnin whoadaay?" Truth greeted.

"Down hurr trappin' and stackin'," Trouble replied.

"Sho you right. Did Dre come through?" Truth questioned.

"Yup cuz, nem doin' good too," Trouble assured.

"Thatz what I wanna hear, how you lookin'?"

Truth tallied all the work Trouble and his crew went through.

"I'm down to a nine piece," he explained.

"Okay, get at me cuz I'm getting low myself."

"Okay cuz."

Truth gave Boss a call next.

"Bruh, what it look like?" Truth questioned.

"Kinda slow fo' some reason," Boss stated while scratching his head.

"I hurr ya, where you at, Fam?" He asked his lieutenant.

"By Raquel's crib eating," Boss stated between chews.

"I'ma ride down on you okay." Truth made him aware.

"Aight."

Truth stepped on the gas, and sped over to Raquel's house.

****

Ding Dong! Ding Dong! Was the sound of Raquel's doorbell.

"I'm comin', I'm comin'! Hold yo' horses, damn!" Raquel yelled as she strutted towards the door in a pair of tight black stretch pants and a pink wife beater.

Raquel was built like Buffy the Body, stood 5'8", had caramel complexed skin and short blonde hair like Nia Long's from the movie Friday. Truth often fantasized on fucking Raquel, but he didn't think he would get away with it. Raquel opened the door after checking her peep hole.

"Hey ugly," Raquel stated, greeting Truth with a hug and smile.

"Hey Sampson," Truth shot back.

Raquel screwed her face up at Truth for his quick come back and reference to her looking like a gorilla.

"Boss in the kitchen with his greedy ass," Raquel chuckled as she flopped down on her couch, turning to the Lifetime Channel.

"What you cook?" Truth asked while undressing Raquel with his eyes.

"Some tacos."

"Bet!"

"Don't carry you greedy ass in there eating errthang up, my kids ain't ate yet," Raquel snapped as she flipped through the cable channels on her bootleg cable.

"Gurl chill, where Jazzie at? I thought y'all were going shopping together," Truth inquired nonchalantly.

Raquel had to think fast because Jazzie told her she went to visit Law.

"Don't tell her I told you this, but I think she went shopping fo' yo' birthday gift," Raquel lied, making sure she didn't make eye contact with Truth.

That was close, she thought.

"I gotcha Raquel, I won't let the cat out the bag," Truth promised as he walked over to Raquel and gave her some dap.

Boss was murdering his food like there was no tomorrow when Truth entered the kitchen.

"Sup," Boss mumbled with a mouth full of food.

"Dem tacos, greedy ass nigga," Truth replied while stalking the plate of food.

"It's plenty of this shit, gone and fix yo'self a plate, nigga. Don't come over here acting brand new and shit," Boss uttered as he bit into his taco.

Truth grabbed a paper plate off the kitchen counter then fixed himself a fat taco.

"What yawl got to drank?"

"I think it's some Corona's or some Kool-Aid in the fridge."

Truth opened the refrigerator then gazed at the bottles of Corona. He wasn't sure if he wanted some sweet Kool-Aid or a cold beer. He decided to go with a cup of Kool-Aid instead, knowing Raquel made it with three different flavors and was always on hit. Raquel's refrigerator stayed fully stocked mainly because Boss always bought food stamps from anybody that was selling them and plugged her.

Truth took a seat at the table then bit into his taco. The shell instantly crumbled, causing the meat, lettuce, cheese, and tomatoes to fall onto the paper plate.

"Damn, yo' gurl can cook, bruh," Truth complimented as he scooped up his taco fillings with his hands.

"I know she gone have a nigga fat as a bitch in a minute," Boss replied as he rubbed on his tight stomach.

"Nigga, yo' girl ain't short stopping either," Boss shot back while sucking on his teeth.

"Well, maybe I'm starving then, bruh," Truth stated as he devoured the rest of his taco.

"Howz business been fo' ya, bruh?" Truth inquired as he took a sip of his Kool-Aid.

"My cousin boyfriend still doing his thang up North and shit. Other than that, I guess I'm aight. Fella was suppose to holla at me 'bout coppin' a few bricks, but I ain't heard from his ass yet," Boss stated.

"What? That nigga was at the wash earlier. He copped three bricks from me," Truth informed Boss.

Truth started to wonder why Fella went behind Boss back to cop instead of dealing with Boss. Boss scratched his head, he was confused.

"So Fella went behind my back and hollered at you? What you tax his ass?" Boss asked while sucking his teeth.

"I taxed him twenty-four G'z for the hard."

"Okay good, cuz I was gone hit him for 23.5," Boss replied with a grin.

"Be careful with dude Truth, I heard he be tryna middle man anybody he can, and you know you don't want everybody in yo' business," Boss stated seriously.

"You right Boss, next time I'ma make sure he hit yo' line cuz I'm sho not tryna be out hurr doing hand to hand deals," Truth replied.

"Okay Fam, thatz what I'm here fo'," Boss stressed as he punched Truth on his shoulder.

"Do you know I ain't heard from Jazzie ass all day?" Truth confessed.

"Maybe she out shopping or something," Boss suggested, trying to convince Truth not to worry.

"I know, thatz what Raquel said. Fuck it, let's go to Red Carpet Lanes tonight, Boss," Truth advised.

"I ain't dressed to go out, Truth," Boss replied as he stared down at himself.

"Shit me neither nigga," Truth shot back.

In reality they were both dressed to go out. Its just they had their outfits on all day.

"I'm driving too Boss, I got the drop outside," Truth stated, trying to make it sound even sweeter knowing Boss loved his drop.

"Cool," Boss replied as he pictured how they would look pulling up in Truth's drop top.

"Grab a zip cuz we gone throw a private powder party afterwards," Truth ordered.

"I like the sound of that, Folks," Boss added as he rubbed his hands quickly.

"We gone have some hoes freak Trouble and Jabar. You know, a lil present for their loyalty to the crew."

Boss stared at Truth as if he was crazy.

"Nigga, you never blessed me like that."

"Cuz we weren't having it like we having it now. Gone and get yo' ass ready, we 'bout to party tonite."

Boss kept some gear at Raquel's house, even though he didn't live there. He scanned through the closet then grabbed a pair of Tommy Hilfiger jeans and shirt.

"Fuck it, might as well put on the socks and cologne too," Boss smiled as he took a seat on Raquel's bed.

Last but not least, Boss laced his feet with some red, blue, and white Nike Air Max 95's, and he debated on wearing his Cartier or Rolex watch.

"Fuck it, I'm going with the Cartier watch with the Cartier frames," Boss uttered as he popped his collar.

Boss went into his stash, retrieved a zip of cocaine and a stack then headed back into the kitchen.

"Where you think you going, nigga?" Raquel asked with an attitude.

"I don't like yo' tone of voice, woman," Boss replied as he pushed Raquel out of his way.

"You just gone eat my food and leave with Truth like I don't exist?" She fumed.

"I done already spent quality time with you and dicked you down, now itz time fo' me to hit the streets," Boss yelled.

"Boss, itz almost midnight!" Raquel cried.

"And!"

The two argued longer. Truth walked towards the door.

"Fuck you trifling ass nigga!" Raquel exploded as she stormed off to her bedroom slamming her door. Boom!

"My fault bruh, yo' azz in the doghouse now," Truth apologized as he burst out laughing.

"Man fuck her, she tryna turn a gangsta into a square ass nigga, Folks," Boss laughed.

"Jazzie be on the same shit. She got mad cuz somebody called me restricted last night," Truth admitted.

"Fam, we sum young hood rich niggaz, we don't need no bitches sweating us over petty shit. We can have any bitch we want. Let's roll before I put hands on dis bitch," Boss fumed as he grabbed his keys off the counter.

Red Carpet Lanes was the hot spot to go, even if you weren't bowling. It had a lounge area for people who wanted to drink or shot pool. Truth and Boss hung at the bowling alley on a regular basis picking up women. They made sure their wifeys never invaded their space, or it would be hell for the chics they were messing with.

Truth flipped his cell phone open then dialed Trouble's number. Bzzz Bzzz Bzzz Bzzzz …

"Damn nigga, answer the phone," Truth mumbled.

"Hello!" Trouble shouted into the phone.

"This Truth, cuz."

"Ahhh, whuzzz zatnin whoaday!"

"Cuz, I need you to get a hotel room at the Hampton Inn, a double bed suite and meet me thurr round 1:30AM."

"K cuz."

"Make sure Jabar thurr too."

"Mane, where you at? It sound like itz jumping in the background?"

"We up at Red Carpet fucking off."

"Boss with cha?"

"Yup."

"Tell that fool I said whut up."

"I gotcha, go get the hotel cuz."

"Aight."

It was packed at Red Carpet Lanes on this particular night. Truth circled around a few times but couldn't find a parking spot.

"You see Fridge parked his Beemer in the handicap spot," Boss pointed out.

"Fuck it, I'll just pay security a few dollaz to look after my shit. Hopefully my shit won't get towed," Truth stated as he stopped in front of the security guards.

Once inside, Truth and Boss did a quick scan of the crowd to peep their surroundings. If an enemy was present they wanted to have the ups on them. After looking around, they decided to relax. The sound system was boomin' so loud that it seemed like the whole building was shaking. Dru Down's song, "Pimp of the Year," was playing in the background while people danced. After squeezing through the thick crowd, Truth and Boss finally made it to the bar.

Truth ordered a bottle of Remy Martin VSOP. Seconds later Pimpin' Rob strolled up to Truth and Boss with three hoes surrounding him. None of his hoes made eye contact with them. They kept their heads down to the floor.

"Whutz hatnin young pimpin'? I see yawl shining like new diamonds. Yawl know me, I'm big tymin'," Pimpin Rob rapped as he leaned to the side.

"You know we tryna get it up, Rob," Truth shot back.

"I can tell you already getting it up. You lil niggaz got on Cartier frames and thangs, these lame niggaz ain't hip."

Everybody burst out laughing and giving each other dap.

"You comin' to my all white birthday bash in Miami, bruh?" Truth asked Pimpin' Rob.

"Nigga, do a pimp wear minks in the winter and slam Cadillac doors on playa hataz!" Pimpin' Rob chanted in his Mac voice.

"Make sure you bring yo' stable cuz itz gone be money floating round that bitch. You know I'm throwing it in a Mansion?"

"Dig dat shit, I told you yawl shining like new diamonds. Be careful in these streets, you know these sucka niggaz will tell on a whale if it'll save they own tail, get in and get the fuck out, remember that, young pimpin', chuurch."

Pimpin' Rob's words sunk into Truth's head as he stated, "Get in and get out, thatz what I'ma do. What you getting into tonight, Rob?"

"I'm tryna catch me some paper."

"Well, stop by the Hampton Inn after the club close and bring yo' hoes, aight."

Rob already knew what time it was. Truth was throwing a powda party. Boss was on the prowl for some fresh meat when suddenly he spotted Shay and her crew posted by the pool tables.

Boss walked up smoothly as he stared the women down.

"How yawl ladies doing tonight?" Boss greeted the women as he rubbed his hands together.

"We good, we good."

"Thatz good to hear."

"We tryna powda our noses tonight, whuz up?" Shay quickly responded.

"Shit, you know how I get down. Yawl can come to the Hampton Inn. We having a powda party, but if yawl ain't fuckin' don't come," Boss stated as he stared directly into Shay's eyes.

"Nigga, we ain't no square ass High School bitches. You know how my crew get down too, just make sure that shit ain't stepped on," Shay shot back as she grabbed Boss' dick.

"Whoaah, simmer down, you gone get to see tha snake."

"Nigga, I'll pull yo' shit out right here and suck it in front of errbody, say I won't," Shay boasted while staring Boss down.

Boss knew Shay would do it because she was bold like that, so he didn't test her.

"Just be at the Hampton Inn and call when yawl in the lobby."

"Okay Folks," Shay purred.

****

It was going down at the Hampton Inn. The ratio was eight to three, favoring the men, exactly the way Truth planned it. Drinks were being poured up, and cocaine was being snorted. None of Truth's crew did coke, but they loved to party with the crowd that did. When Truth was on the come up, this is how he made his money outside of trapping out of his trap house. It was a lot of money to be made at the after hours, and cocaine was always in high demand.

"Shay, you enjoying yo'self?" Boss asked with a sneaky grin.

"Most def fam, when you gone let a bitch taste that there?" Shay flirted as she grabbed Boss' dick and licked her lips.

"Not tonight, I need yawl to take care of my nigga, Jabar, and don't be easy on him," Boss instructed as he rubbed Shay pussy print.

"Okay Boss, anything fo' you, but you owe me fo' this, and I'm coming to collect afterwards."

Shay ran her fingers over Boss' chest then licked the side of his face.

Man, I would beat her pussy up if this would've been any other night, Boss thought to himself while grinning.

Shay and her crew walked over to Jabar, who was smoking a blunt on the couch minding his business. Jabar had no idea what was in store for him as the women approached him gyrating slowly in front of him. Jabar smiled as he blew weed smoke into the air. He enjoyed the show the women were putting on in front of him. He put his blunt down and focused all his attention towards the women.

"Rob, I see you came through fo' yo' boy," Truth smiled as he gave Pimpin' Rob some dap.

"I keeps my word, Truth, thatz all I got, especially if I fucks with cha. So whatz good, pimpin'?"

"I want all yo' hoes to freak my lil cuz, Trouble," Truth informed Pimpin' Rob as he grinned.

Pimpin' Rob smiled as he rubbed his chin, "You freaky muhfucka you."

The two men laughed.

"He ain't never experienced no shit like that, so I had to bless him, ya dig?"

"Well, you know my hoes don't fuck fo' free, Fam."

"I know the game, Rob. They can keep the rest of that powder, and here," Truth pulled out a stack then stared at Rob.

"If you wasn't my nigga I'd smack that out yo' hand, but since you certified, I'ma keep it pimpin'."

"My nigga," Truth replied as he gave Rob some dap.

Trouble and Jabar were the center of attention as the women put on a show. Niggaz were making it rain and trying to buy pussy, but tonight was all about the Lil G'z. It started to get hot and steamy as clothes started coming off, and the haters started to surface.

"Bitch, you ain't shit, yo' hair fake anyway," one of the haters snapped.

"That's why you sitting there with a hard dick nigga," one of Pimpin' Rob's hoes shot back.

"I run through hoes like yawl and pass 'em to my workers," the hater bragged.

"Nigga, shut yo' sorry ass up, driving a damn '82 Chevy, nigga. Get yo' weight up fo' you try to down grade a thoroughbred, bitch."

"Bitch, I'll slap the taste out yo' mouth!" The hater snapped as he stared at his boys.

"And I'll snatch the life up out yo' bitch ass," Pimpin' Rob barked as he rose up from his chair.

"Is errthang aight, Rob?" Truth interjected.

"Nah Fam, we got a hater over here blockin' on one of my bitches," Pimpin Rob explained while gritting his teeth.

"Oh fo' real," Truth replied.

Truth walked up to the hater and cracked him over the head with a Remy Martin bottle. Pimpin' Rob started stomping the hater as blood gushed all over the carpet as everybody gazed in amazement. Nobody tried to stop the beating. They just stared and shook their heads.

After they felt they did enough damage to the hater, they stripped him down to his boxers and socks then took his car keys and kicked him out of the suite. Everything went back to normal afterwards.

"That bitch ass nigga tried to fuck up my night, bruh," Trouble stated.

"Huh bruh, I feel like Hugh Hefner over hurr," Jabar shot back as he was getting blowed and licked on.

"You sho' dem niggaz can handle all that pussy, Truth?" Boss joked.

"They betta cuz I paid fo' these bitches," Truth shot back with a smile.

"Okay, since we got rid of that fuck nigga, let's finish this night off like playaz," Pimpin' Rob announced as he grabbed his glass of Remy Martin.

Before they knew it, every bitch in the hotel was on their knees blowing all the niggaz.

Boss and Truth tag teamed one bitch and was giving it to her like real porn stars. This is how powder parties always ended. What Truth and Boss didn't know was their girlfriends occasionally threw powder parties from time to time, but they hired male strippers for entertainment. They kept their parties a tight lipped secret amongst themselves because they knew if they didn't there would be serious repercussions.

Chapter 8

Truth needed to reup, so he got in contact with Joel. He increased the order to thirty bricks since his squad was running through the them so quickly. Truth figured he was close enough to his goal and could exit the game after this last flip. Truth had two million dollars in cold hard cash stashed away, plus a couple front businesses.

Truth was starting to become extremely paranoid as the days passed. He had his suspicions about Jazzie fucking off on him, but he didn't have any concrete evidence to confront her. Truth continued to shower Jazzie with money and lavish gifts. Jazzie continued to send money to Law. She felt guilty about breaking bad on him and figured that money would get her back in good graces with Law. Law continued to stack every dime so that he could pay for his legal defense for his appeal.

Meanwhile, Yusef sent word back to Boss about seeing Jazzie on a visit with Law. Boss wasn't sure how he should handle the situation. He knew how much Truth loved Jazzie and would probably kill her. He applied pressure to Raquel to find out everything he could about Jazzie

and Law's situation. Raquel tried her best not to snitch on her cousin, but Boss threatened to cut her off financially, so she quickly weighed her options. She suddenly broke down and began spilling her guts while bursting into tears. Raquel couldn't believe she sold her best friend of fifteen years out for her own personal gain.

"How long this bullshit been goin' on!" Boss snapped as he pounded his fist on the dining room table demanding an explanation.

Raquel was trembling like a wet cat, "B-b-b- 'bout four months," Raquel stuttered as snot gushed from her nostril.

"Damn! She a dirty ass bitch!" Boss snapped as his blood began to boil. "I gotta tell my nigga, but how do I break this shit to him?" Boss pondered.

Boss' friendship with Truth started way before the dope game, and they always had each other's back. As a man, Boss felt obligated to protect his friend, he didn't like the fact that he was sleeping with the enemy or better yet a frenemy. Boss decided to break the news to Truth after his party. He didn't want to ruin his moment.

Damn, I hope he don't kill the bitch though, Boss thought to himself. But if he does, she deserved it, death before dishonor, if you ain't with us then you damn sho against us, Boss thought as he stared at Raquel wishing she would try to snake him.

****

"Whuz good Truth?" Baby Drew uttered in his thick syrupy southern drawl.

"Money, hoes and clothes," Truth replied while staring at the wall display of CD's at Audio Vibe record store.

"Why you ain't tell me 'bout yo' party in Miami, Folks?" Baby Drew asked.

"I ain't have yo' number, bruh."

"Why you ain't ride down on me in the hood then, fam?"

Truth cracked a smile, knowing he could've easily rode down on Baby Drew.

"You right bruh, my bad, you should come down and perform," Truth invited.

"I gotcha Folks, I can promote my new CD "Powder" while I'm down thurr, that bitch bangin' too," Baby Drew stated confidently as he rubbed his chin and grinned.

Truth grabbed UGK's CD "Riding Dirty," then flipped it over so that he could read the song credits.

"When you suppose to drop that bitch, bruh?" Truth inquired.

"'Round Christmas. I wanna promote it some mo' before I drop it though," Drew explained.

"You ain't wrong bruh, you ain't wrong. I need an advance copy of that muh fucka once yo' drop. I'll pay for it too. I know it cost to put that shit together," Truth stated.

"Mane bruh, you ain't gotta pay fo' a CD, you my folks. But what you can do is book me a studio session with yo' bruh, dat nigga got sum fire ass beats," Baby Drew pointed out.

Truth couldn't help but smile after hearing Drew praise his brother's production skills.

"I gotcha. Next year we gone launch our own label, we setting up shop in Atlanta too. If yo' situation ain't working fo' you give me a holla."

"Thanks bruh, you know I'ma loyal nigga though, but if yawl need some features I'll hop on sum tracks with no prob'," Baby Drew countered as he gave Truth some dap.

Truth walked over to the checkout counter after wrapping up things with Baby Drew.

"Whuz new thatz actually bangin', fam?" Trust asked the store clerk. "I see you already got that new UGK in yo' hands. I got that Face Mob, Master P new shit, "Ice Cream Man," Do or Die "Po' Pimpin'", and Mr. Mike "Wicked Ways.""

Truth cut the store clerk off in mid sentence.

"Give me all those CD's and the Source Magazine," Truth requested eagerly.

The store clerk popped in a CD he knew Truth hadn't heard yet then grinned. Once the beat kicked in, Truth started bobbing his head.

"First of all, fuck the click and tha bitch you claim!" Tupac vented menacingly out of the speakers.

"Thatz my nigga, Pac! When this shit come out!" Truth spurted frantically.

"Today," the clerk informed.

"I see you holdin' out on me, cuz," Truth replied with a grin.

The store clerk was grinning from ear to ear as Truth stared at him.

"We ain't suppose to sell new releases 'til Tuesday," the clerk explained.

"Mane bruh, I'll pay twenty dollars fo' that CD. You can even give me the one in the CD player and keep the case."

The store clerk thought about it for a second.

"Act like it," he shot back, knowing he was gone pocket the money anyway.

Truth paid for all the CD's plus gave the clerk an extra twenty.

"Nice doing business with cha," Truth stated.

"Nah, nice doing business with you," the store clerk replied.

"Next year my brother CD's and posters gone line yo' walls, so make sure you show us some love, bruh," Truth beamed.

"Who Future?" The clerk wondered.

"Yessir," Truth confirmed.

"I can't wait cuz I heard he a beast," the clerk replied.

"He is, bruh, he is," Truth agreed with the clerk as he grabbed his bags.

Truth immediately popped the Tupac CD in his deck then cranked the system all the way up. He was so geeked he started bouncing around frantically. Truth slapped his car in drive then checked his rear view. He needed to bust a U-Turn, so he patiently waited for traffic to clear up before pulling off. Once traffic was clear, he made a sharp left turn towards the middle of the island then waited for his chance to merge into traffic going east.

The haters they smashed at the hotel was riding shotgun with one of his goons in a '84 Monte Carlo down Capital Dr. when they spotted Truth stuck in traffic.

"Slow down fam, there go that nigga Truth," the hater uttered.

Just so happened JaBar and Trouble were coming down Capital Dr. too. They spotted Truth trying to bust a U-Turn, so they slowed down. The hater and his flunky rolled up on Truth, catching him off guard. The hater suddenly rose from the passenger side window with his gun in hand then started squeezing shots at Truth.

Trouble gunned his car over the island, ramming the back bumper of the shooter's Monte Carlo. Instantly JaBar hopped out with his twin Glock 40's airing the shooters car up, Whawk!

Whawk! Whawk! Whawk! Whawk! JaBar wasn't playing with these clowns as he emptied the clip relentlessly. A mini car pileup happened when the driver of a 1990 Buick Lesabre slammed on her brakes. The sounds of car tires screeching blared as the bullets ripped through the thick sheet metal. Truth mashed down hard on his gas pedal trying to break free of the mayhem that was taking place.

Everything happened so fast, Truth's heart was racing. He thought about how quickly his life could have ended. Ambulance and police sirens echoed from miles away as they raced towards the scene of the shooting. Unfortunately, it was too late for the ambulance to save the shooters in the Monte Carlo, JaBar killed them both. The driver was slumped over on the steering wheel, causing the horn to blare nonstop.

The victims' bodies were riddled with bullets, blood splattered all over the windshield, like the saying goes, "you live by the gun, you die by the gun." Unfortunately, these two victims hadn't anticipated on leaving this earth on this very day. Trouble gunned his trap car down 23rd, made a right then hit Teutonia Ave. Next, he made a left turn on Atkinson Ave. headed towards the Eastside. Truth pulled over once he felt he was in the clear. His heart was racing as he tried to make some sense out of what just happened.

"Damn, them bitches could've took my head off," he snapped.

Moments later his cell phone started ringing.

"Cuz, you aight? We had to murk dem hoe azz niggaz!" Trouble boasted while breathing heavily.

"That was yawl dumpin' back thurr?" Truth replied.

"Yeah mane, dem niggaz crept up on you from behind when you was trying to bust that U-Turn on 23rd thinking it was sweet and got they fool ass aired out!" Trouble stated coldly.

Truth was grateful Trouble and JaBar were there to save his life. He vowed he would make sure Trouble and JaBar made it to the top in the dope game. Truth stared up at the sky and locked his fingers as he prayed.

"Thank you Lord for sparing me, I don't know what I would do without you," he whispered as he sighed heavily.

****

Jazzie continued to visit Law. She figured since she got caught, wasn't no point in stopping now.

"I go to court in a few weeks for my appeal hearing. If I loose, I got some dirt on this dirty cop, Detective Bryant," Law whispered to Jazzie.

"Bryant? He on suspension indefinitely without pay. Him and his partner were dope dating, and some niggaz taped it then tossed they ass in the trunk, so his credibility is shot," Jazzie informed Law.

"Word, word, my lawyer said he had a trump card, didn't know he was talking 'bout that," Law replied with a big smile on his face.

"So you think you gone loose the initial appeal?" Jazzie asked.

"Honestly, I don't know. But if I do, all this dirt we got should get my case over turned. I'm trying to come home and beat that pussy up," Law joked as he rubbed on Jazzie's swollen mound. "You still love me Jazzie?" Law asked as he gazed into Jazzie eyes.

Jazzie thought for a second before replying, "Yes, why?"

"I just wanna know."

"Do you think I'd be visiting you if I didn't and got a nigga at home?" Jazzie shot back without blinking.

"I know that. I asked cuz you know when I come home I'm gone be fucked up and gone need some paper ASAP."

"So what that gotta do with me, Law? You know that money I been sending you is money Truth been giving me."

Law rubbed his chin as he grinned then stared at the floor.

"I want you to peel that nigga safe when I get out so we'll have enough money to start a new life," Law ordered as the smile on his face turned into a frown.

Jazzie was astonished by what Law just suggested.

"And how am I suppose to pull that off? I don't know where he keep his money," Jazzie countered.

"That's yo' job to find out, dumb bitch. You sleep with the nigga errday. When I get released you better have a 100G'z waiting for me, or I'm gone put something in yo' life and I guarantee you won't like it. Remember you in the rear, you still owe me," Law whispered as he squeezed Jazzie's wrist tightly.

The pain was excruciating. Jazzie's face started to instantly turned red.

"Let me go, you hurting me," Jazzie whimpered.

"Bitch, you better do as I said and strip that nigga. I gotta have mines by all means," Law instructed as he loosened up the grip on Jazzie's wrist.

Jazzie dropped her head as her stomach started bubbling. She tried to fathom the thought of robbing Truth for Law. It was definitely a suicide mission. Jazzie started to regret feeling sorry for Law and reaching out to him. She was no longer a hoe. She was now Truth's wifey and ride or die bitch. All she had to do was maintain the house, fuck Truth good, and make sure his Salon ran smooth. She knew if she went back to Law she'd be subject to his emotional and physical abuse, which is something she dreaded.

As the visit came to an end, all Jazzie could think about was how Law saved her life when they first met. When she was seventeen, Jazzie worked for a pimp by the name of Sunny Gibbs. At that point in her life, Jazzie was a lost soul, looking for guidance.

Jazzie was raped by her uncle when she was fifteen. He threatened to kill her if she ever told anyone. Jazzie didn't doubt that he would follow through on his threat, but she felt that her mother had to know about her brother's devilish act. Once she built up enough courage to confide in her mother, she got the surprise of her life. Her mother snapped. She slapped Jazzie so hard she fell to the floor then accused her of lying. Jazzie was called every filthy name her mother could think of. Jazzie was in total shock as she stared back at her mother.

"My brother would never do no sick shit like this, lil bitch!! Yo' lil hot ass probably mad he didn't want to fuck yo' nasty ass!! You know what!! Pack yo' shit and get the fuck out my house. I'm sick of looking at yo' nasty lying ass, and I know you been fucking niggaz when I be at work." Jazzie had a confused look on her face. In an instant, her face turned hard as her mother's word cut threw her flesh. "Bitch, did you hear me? Get the fuck out my house!!!"

Jazzie slowly rose to her feet while cutting her eyes at her mother. I hope you die from AIDs, bitch. I wouldn't show up to yo' funeral, she thought. Jazzie bounced around from house to house 'til one day she met the man of her dreams.

****

Jazzie was at a powder party when some tricks tried propositioning her for some pussy. She was exhausted from all the tricks she serviced earlier in the day. Jazzie shot all of their offers down, which was a major violation. One trick got so pissed at Jazzie he figured he'd get her back by telling her pimp, Sunny, on her. Turning down money was a major violation, and he knew there would be some serious repercussions for Jazzie behind this.

"Hey Sunny, let me wrap with you for a sec. Dig this here, I tried to buy some pussy from yo' hoe bitch Jazzie, and the bitch shot a nigga down."

Sunny Gibbs lifted his face up from the plate of cocaine then wiped his nose.

"A bitch did what! Run dat by me again, I don't think I heard you correctly."

"Sunny, I tried to pay fo' pussy from yo' hoe bitch Jazzie. The bitch said she too tired and told me to move around," the trick explained.

"I know my bitch ain't turned down nann dolla! Where that silly bitch at!" Sunny snapped.

"She at the bar, Sunny," the trick replied with a big grin.

Sunny had a reputation for putting a foot in his bitch's ass. By him being amongst players and pimps, he had to demonstrate how he puts it down on an out of line hoe. Sunny rose from his chair with his pimp cane in one hand and his pimp cup in the other. He walked up to Jazzie, tapped her on the shoulder then struck her in the back of the head with his pimp cup spilling all his Cognac and knocking her to the floor. Jazzie looked up at Sunny with tears in her eyes.

"Daddy, what you doing?" Jazzie cried.

"Bitch, you don't question a pimp! What you doing turning down money like this shit a game! You shut the fuck up and turn these tricks. Thank itz a game or something, bitch!"

Without warning, Sunny raised his Ostrich boot up then slammed it down on Jazzie's head. He called her every name he could think of as blood gushed all over the floor. The stench of fresh shit lingered throughout the air. Jazzie couldn't hold it in any longer.

"Bitch! When you started thanking fo' yo'self, huh! Bitch, my lifestyle too damn expensive for yo' ass to be turning money down!"

"D- D- Dad…"

Sunny whacked Jazzie across the face before she could finish her sentence.

"Bitch, I do all the thinking fo' you! You don't say shit unless a pimp tell you to!"

"Please Daddy, I was tired," Jazzie whined.

"Bitch, ain't no fringe benefits in this here game! I run this shit! If I say you on break, you go on break!"

Sunny raised his pimp cane and started whacking Jazzie viciously across her body. Jazzie screamed loudly from the atrocious pain. Jazzie was slowly loosing her consciousness when out of nowhere Law came to her rescue.

"Stop beating her, pimpin'. You done proved yo' point," Law stated as he intervened.

"Nigga, don't try to tell me how to discipline my bitch, fuck you thank you is, Captain Save A Hoe, nigga?" Sunny snapped.

Law and Sunny had a brief stare down, both men didn't blink.

"I'ma a mutha fuckin gangsta nigga, and don't ever disrespect me like that again, or I'm gone show you how I getz down," Law stated aggressively.

Sunny pushed his hair out his face then stared at Law unveiling a devilish grin.

"So you making threats, bitch ass nigga?"

Soon as Law heard the words "Bitch ass nigga," he slapped Sunny with so much force Sunny spun around like Michael Jackson and fell to the floor. Law pulled his snub nose .38 out and squeezed three shots into Sunny; one in the shoulder, groin, and knee cap.

"You lucky I ain't kill you, nigga. I'm just gone take yo' bitch and make you watch her get money fo' me trick," Law uttered as he spit in Sunny's face.

Sunny was laying in a puddle of his own blood squirming like a fish on shore as the niggaz at the powder party was in aww at what just transpired. Sunny was in grave pain and was slowly loosing consciousness. He didn't know if he would live or not.

Jazzie's eyes slowly cracked open, she scanned the room wondering where she was at. While she was unconscious, Law bathed and cleaned her up. He saw potential in Jazzie and was ready to get her back working. Jazzie thought to herself, God must've heard my prayers.

****

Tears slid down Jazzie's face as vivid images of the assault she suffered flashed through her mind. She had no idea she was being followed and videotaped. She would soon find out what's done in the dark will soon come to the light.

****

Truth had a 20K day. His pager started booming at 9AM and been going hard ever since. He had every intention on stopping to get something to eat, but the money keep calling him. Truth had the taste for some Chinese food. He figured he'd wait 'til later and take Jazzie out for dinner. He flipped his cell phone open then gave Jazzie a call. Bzzz Bzzz Bzzz Bzzzz, was the sound of Jazzie cell phone as it vibrated on the passenger seat. She stared down at it debating on whether or not she should answer it, fearing it might be Truth.

"Fuck it," Jazzie mumbled as she answered the call. "Hello," Jazzie stated calmly.

"Hey Jaz," Truth replied seductively in his syrupy southern voice.

Jazzie prepared to explain her whereabouts, knowing that would be Truth's next question.

"Where you at?" Truth asked.

"Coming from Gurnee Mills with Raquel. We was bored so we decided to go shopping."

"Oh, okay. How long you gone be fo' you make it back?"

"About forty-five minutes," Jazzie lied, assuming if she picked up speed she'd actually be back in town by then.

"Okay, I'm tryna go to La Joy's tonight, you down?" Truth inquired.

"You know I am. I ain't cooking tonight no way," Jazzie countered with a big smile.

"Well, I'll save you a seat, so just meet me up thurr. I'ma wait forty-five minutes before I leave though."

"Okay Daddy." After the call ended Jazzie exhaled deeply, "This shit is getting out of hand. I can't wait 'til itz all over with."

Jazzie tossed her phone on the passenger seat then floored her Corvette down the hwy, trying to get back to Milwaukee asap.

Truth figured since he just had an attempt on his life, he might as well squad up just in case somebody tried him again. He went home and threw on his bullet proof vest. He grabbed his twin HK . 45 Semi Auto's then kissed them both. Trouble was breaking down a bag of dro when his phone started vibrating.

"JaBar answer dat fo' me," Trouble commanded.

"Who dis?" JaBar asked.

"Rick James bitch!"

"Huh bruh?"

"Nigga, this Truth, whuzz zatnin, folks?" Truth joked.

"Shit," JaBar replied with a slight chuckle. "Where Trouble at?"

"Rollin a bliggity."

"Tell him to meet me at La Joy's tonight. I'm paying, so bring yawl hungry asses," Truth ordered.

"I'm wit' dat bruh, plus it be some bitches up thurr."

"Well, meet me up thurr in a hour then."

"Aight Truth, we'll be thurr."

"Who was dat, bruh?" Trouble asked as he licked the blunt then sealed it.

"Truth. He said meet him at La Joy's in a hour. He buying us dinner."

"Huh bruh, I'm hungry ass a sorry hoe too," Trouble joked.

"Shiidd, I am too nigga," JaBar shot back.

"We can roll up thurr, but first we gotta get our smoke on then put this money up," Trouble grinned as he placed the flame up to his freshly rolled blunt.

Truth's next move was to call his head lieutenant, Boss. Bzzz Bzzz Bzzzz Bzzz, was the sound of Boss' cell phone as it danced on the dining room table. Boss was flicking through the cable channels while scratching his balls. He had no intentions on moving an inch of his bones.

"Pass me my phone, Raquel!" Boss commanded.

"I ain't yo' maid, nigga!" Raquel screamed back with her mouth poked out.

"Shut up bitch!"

This a ol' disrespectful ass nigga, Raquel thought as she handed Boss the phone.

"Who dis?" Boss asked as he cut his eye at Raquel. "You lucky I don't smack the black off yo' smart mouth ass," Boss whispered.

"Whatever," Raquel mumbled as she turned and strutted off to the kitchen.

"This Truth East, whuzz zatnin with cha?"

"Shit, sitting here flicking threw channels and arguing with Raquel punk ass." Boss complained.

Raquel was cussing up a storm in the background. Truth thought it was amusing. "Ain't shit funny, Truth," Boss shot back seriously.

"Simmer down my nigga, she gone fuck around and Al Green yo' ass."

"I wish that bitch would, I'll be in county jail facing homicide charges on the G."

After getting his laughs in, Truth's attitude quickly changed.

"Bruh, I just talked to Jazzie, and she said she was with Raquel! The bitch said they on they way back from Gurnee Mills!"

"Fo' real fam?"

"Yeah bruh, ol' lying ass heffa!"

"Calm down, Folks, calm down. Maybe itz a logical explanation to all this," Boss reasoned as he tried to calm Truth down.

"Fuck that! This bitch on some sheisty shit. I just told her to meet me at La Joy's. Should I have you bring Raquel up thurr so I can catch her azz up or just play with her head to see what she was on?" Truth asked as he wiped his greasy face.

Boss thought for a second before responding to Truth's question.

"Play her lil game Folks, cuz I don't wanna have her and Raquel fallin' out over this, ya feel me?"

"I feel ya bruh, that's what I'm gone do. I thank I'm gone head to Miami tomorrow night so I can get a head start on my party arrangements. You gone roll out with me or fly down later?"

"Who said I was flying? I'm driving, so yeah I'ma head out tomorrow." Boss thought about the long drive then reality slapped him in the face. "I'ma fly East, I forgot how long that drive was. I don't know what the hell I was thinking."

"Well, I'll hit you up tomorrow then."

"Okay Folks, be safe. Trouble told me what happened with dem niggaz tryna air you out."

Truth's thoughts went back to the attempt on his life.

"Mane bruh, that was a close call too," Truth replied as he inhaled then exhaled slowly.

"Truth, you a hood legend. I think you need to be preparing for yo' departure from the game, Folks, real talk," Boss voiced, giving Truth his perspective.

Boss' words hit Truth like a ton of bricks. Deep down he knew Boss was telling the truth, but accepting it was a hard pill to swallow.

"How much paper you got put away. Boss?" Truth asked out of curiousity.

"Why?" Boss replied with a confused look on his face.

"Because I wanna know that you straight if I ever decide to walk away."

Boss sat in silence for a moment as he wondered if he really wanted his best friend to call it quits.

"One more month and I'll be at a quarter mill, fam. That should be enough dough for me to start a business."

If I got a few Mill I gotta make sure Boss sitting on a million before I call it quits. It's only right, Truth thought to himself.

"Boss, we like Mike and Scottie, I'm not ready to leave the game just yet. It's sweet as bear meat out chea, we might as well get it while the getting is good," Truth insisted.

Boss' face lit up after hearing Truth hustlaz speech.

"My nigga, we all we got."

"Money over bitches."

"In that order, my G."

Truth hung up the phone then thought about how he would play Jazzie. He knew she was up to something but couldn't place his finger on it.

****

Truth pulled into La Joy's then parked in a handicap spot. He scanned the scene looking for anything that looked suspect. Truth kept his music on as he stuffed one of his pistols inside his waist. He figured it would be best to wait inside his car 'til JaBar and Trouble showed up, just in case the funk jumped off again.

Tupac's song, "Me against the World" was playing in the background as Truth began to reflect on how his life and how it was spiraling out of control. He knew deep inside he needed to slow down or he would wind up six feet deep pushing up daisies or locked in the pen with Buck Roger numbers.

"As soon as we get back from Miami, I should cancel Jazzie ass," Truth grumbled, then reality hit him in the face.

Truth remembered Jazzie played a major role in his sudden rise in the game, and dropping her wouldn't be a smart move. Trouble's booming car system could be heard blocks away. The thunderous bass caught Truth's attention as Trouble pulled into the parking lot bobbing his head and setting off car alarms. Trouble parked his whip then grabbed his iron from under the seat. Truth hopped out of his whip then hit the button on his car alarm.

"Whuz zatnin whoaday?" Trouble greeted.

"Not much cuz, just ready to get my eat and drank on," Truth replied.

"Huh bruh, I want a Tropical Itch, them muh fuckaz get a nigga right," Trouble laughed.

"Them bitches be having my ass on lean," JaBar added while grabbing his crotch.

As they entered La Joy's, they made a mental note of everybody inside the restaurant, making sure none of their enemies were lurking in the cut. It wasn't unlikely to run across a rival inside La Joy's. Niggaz from every set frequented the restaurant on a regular basis. Truth, Trouble, and JaBar were all packing burners and had on body armor. They knew in the streets anything could happen at any given moment.

"Ahhh Truth! How you been my brudda?" The Thai restaurant manager greeted in her native tongue.

"I been good Ming Li," Truth replied as he extended his hand out for a handshake.

After the brief greeting, they were escorted to their table then handed menus. The men already knew what they wanted to drink, so they ordered them immediately.

"Bring us three Tropical Itch's and a Mai Tai," Truth requested.

"Okay, I'll be right back with your drinks," Ming Li replied.

Truth and Ming Li were very cool with each other. Ming Li knew when Truth stopped by the restaurant, he was gone spend a nice piece of change. She also had a secret crush on him.

Jazzie arrived just as the drinks were being delivered.

"Hey Trouble, JaBar, Babe," Jazzie stated as she took a deep breath and sat down.

"Hey Jazzie," Trouble and JaBar replied at the same time.

Jazzie kissed Truth on the lips, got herself situated then took a sip of her Mai Tai.

Everybody was buzzing at the table after a few drinks. The liquor got the best of Trouble, so he excused himself from the table. His bladder felt like it was about to burst. Trouble stumbled into the men's room, almost bumping into somebody leaving out. The Tropical Itch definitely took its toll on him.

JaBar was on a hoe hunt. Luckily, he spotted something he liked right away. He was feeling himself tonight, so he excused himself from the table also. The table was now clear. Truth tried his best to act like nothing was bothering him.

"So what you buy today, Jaz?" Truth asked, trying to get a conversation going.

"Huh?" Jazzie replied, looking dumfounded.

"Didn't you go to Gurnee Mills today?" Truth interrogated as he locked his fingers.

"Oh, just some stuff," Jazzie replied dryly.

Truth knew from Jazzie's response she was hiding something, so he switched the subject.

Detective Bryant was sitting at the bar downing shots of Jack Daniels. After his last shot, he spun around in his bar stool and spotted Truth and Jazzie. Detective Bryant was pretty wasted, so he rubbed his eyes to make sure his eyes weren't playing tricks on him. Truth was explaining the shoot out to Jazzie, but she wasn't listening because she had to pee real bad. Jazzie's feet was tapping rapidly on the floor as she waited for Truth to finish his sentence.

"I gotta use the bathroom, babe, hold that thought."

"Don't forget to wipe the seat before you sit down," Truth joked.

"Fuck you Truth," Jazzie shot back as she gave him the middle finger.

Jazzie grabbed her purse then strutted off towards the ladies room turning heads as she passed by. Jazzie was so focused on getting to the ladies room that she didn't notice Detective Bryant sitting at the bar. As she approached Detective Bryant's path, he snatched her by the arm.

"Hey cunt, I see we meet again," Detective Bryant stated in a drunken slur.

Jazzie tried to snatch her arm away from him, but he had a firm grip on her. Detective Bryant reeked of liquor and cheap cologne. Jazzie turned her face away from him, trying to avoid the unpleasant smell.

"Let me go bastard!" Jazzie demanded.

"Fuck you. Let me ask you a lil question. I hear through the grape vine Law has some dirt on me and plans on getting me indicted to save his ass. Is this true?" Detective Bryant asked as he grit his teeth together.

"I don't know what you're talking about, let me go!" Jazzie snapped as she tried to free her arm from Detective Bryant's grip.

"Bitch stop playing, you know what I'm talking about. You been going to visit Law, right?" Jazzie shook her head. "Don't lie!"

"I said no! What, you following me now?"

Detective Bryant smiled revealing his coffee stained teeth. He leaned forward and whispered into Jazzie's ear.

"You'd be surprised who I know, and I bet Truth don't know you stepping out on him, do he?"

Jazzie mustered all her strength together then hit Detective Bryant over the head with her purse. Security noticed the commotion, so they ran over to make sure Jazzie was okay. Truth watched the incident unfold from his table. He stared at Detective Bryant wondering, Why he keep harassing Jazzie? Truth got up to see what the deal was.

"Is errthang okay partna?"

Detective Bryant ice grilled Truth as he let out a low chuckle.

"I was just admiring the young lady's shoes. I love how she wearing them with her outfit," Detective Bryant stated coldly as he rubbed his chin. "Truth, I think you need to keep a leash on this pussy cat cuz it tends to stray," Detective Bryant suggested as he raised his shirt revealing his Colt 45.

Truth had a menacing look on his face as he stared Detective Bryant down.

"Who is you to tell me how to handle minez, chump? You need to be tending to yo' den after getting caught dope dating and trunked in yo' own car. You the last person I'd take advice from."

Truth's words cut through Detective Bryant's skin like a rusty box cutter. He couldn't think of a fast enough reply, so he dispersed from the scene. Truth still had no idea Detective Bryant was the one behind the drive by a month ago. At this point all he wanted to know was what he said to Jazzie.

"What this all about, Jazzie!" Truth asked with aggression.

Jazzie couldn't think of a good enough lie.

"I don't know! He think I know something 'bout Rudy's death!"

Truth was raging with anger as he stared at Jazzie.

"What you tell him! Don't lie neither!" Truth grilled.

"Nothing! Nothing Truth! I let him do all the talking."

A tear drop slowly slid down Jazzie's cheek bone, she was clearly putting on a show.

"You did good, baby," Truth stated as he gently wiped the tears away from her cheek then gave her a hug. "Cheer up lil momma, we still got my party to look forward to. You ready to roll out tomorrow?"

"Y-Y-Yeah," Jazzie stuttered.

"Well, let's get the fuck out of hurr."

****

The following day everyone packed their bags and headed to Mitchell International Airport. Trouble and JaBar had never flown before, so they were petrified something might happen.

"Say Truth, we bet not crash. I ain't with this flying shit," Boss stressed nervously.

"I ain't with this flying shit neither, Boss," Trouble replied as Jabar agreed.

"Mane, yawl niggaz pussy, just go to the bar and slam a couple shots so yawl scary asses can relax. Can't believe this shit. Yawl mo' likely to die on the highway then from a plane crash," Truth noted as he shook his head at his scared crew.

Boss, Trouble, and JaBar took Truth's advice and rushed over to the bar to take a few shots to the head. Truth had to handle some business, so he flipped his cell phone open and called his Lawyer, Joel Fletcher.

"Hey Joel, this Truth."

"Hey!" Joel replied excitedly.

"I'm at the airport heading down to Miami, make sure you call your friend at that exotic car dealership and let him know I'm coming down. I think I'm looking to cop a Dodge Viper."

"Don't worry Truth, I got you. Once you find your car give me a call, and I'll handle all the paperwork. So stop worrying and enjoy your weekend, and pleeeeeease, please take care of the mansion," Joel begged.

"I will mane, you got my word. I'll holla at you later, Joel," Truth promised.

"Don't fuck up the mansion, Truth. I swear if you do, our relationship is over," Joel replied.

"Aight I understand, now stop worrying Joel," Truth sighed.

Jazzie and Raquel decided to grab a few drinks before boarding the plane. While at the bar, Jazzie confessed to Raquel about all the drama in her life, not knowing Raquel already told Boss all her business. As they walked back to the departure area, Raquel grabbed Jazzie hand.

"Girl, you got a soap opera goin' on. I couldn't stand in yo' shoes for ten minutes."

The ladies sat and talked more. Jazzie dropped her head then took a deep breath.

"I know girl, I don't know what to do either. Law might be getting out soon too. The pressure really gone be on then, Raquel," she admitted with shame.

"Girl, no matter what happens I'll have yo back," Raquel assured Jazzie.

"Thanks cuz," Jazzie stated as she cracked a slight smile.

Raquel returned the smile as she caressed Jazzie's hand.

"Let's stop feeling sorry fo' ourselves and party our asses off, now smile bitch."

****

Once they made it to Miami, they caught a cab to the Tuscan Villa. The mansion was located on South Beach with a gorgeous view and lush landscaping. The Tuscan Villa was 5500 sq ft., with five bedrooms and four baths. The amenities included a bay view, easy wide bay access, dockage, Olympic sized pool, Jacuzzi, billiard rooms, wet bar, gourmet kitchen, and luxury master suite with luxury bath. All the furniture was imported from Italy and was truly beautiful.

Fine pieces of artwork adorned the spacious wall resembling a museum. Gucci rugs were placed on the floor to match the Gucci comforters. From the looks of it you'd think an NBA player lived in the Tuscan Villa. Inside the four car garage there were a 1994 Mercedes Benz 500 SEL, A '68 Camaro, a '95 Jaguar Van De Plas, and a few ATV's. Truth and his crew were in awe of what their eyes were witnessing.

"Damn, now this is how I wanna live, yawl!" Truth yelled out.

"Huh bruh, I feel like we in a rap video," Trouble uttered.

"I'm feelin' this folks, you showed yo' ass this time, on the G," Boss testified.

Truth was basking in the glory. He gazed at the estate then grinned.

"Jazzie, call the caterer and get everything in order, I want things to be perfect," he instructed.

"Okay babe," Jazzie agreed.

"We gotta a lot to do today, yawl. Once Jazzie done with the caterer, I gotta get to this exotic car dealership so I can pick out my birthday present," Truth stated with excitement.

"Damn Folks, you bullshitting right?" Boss laughed.

"Don't believe me, just watch. I'm 'bout to act a donkey," Truth swore confidently.

"I'm going too!" Jazzie whined in her baby voice.

A stretch Lincoln town car pulled up into the drive way ready to transport the crew. The Limo was stocked with an assortment of high quality liquor. Boss wasted no time, he started pouring everybody a glass of Giacomo Conterno's Barolo Monfortino.

"Let's make a toast to the birthday boy! We've come a long way in such a short time. Who would've ever imagined we would be setting foot inside a mansion in Miami? To Truth, happy birthday!"

The sound of wine flutes clicking against each other echoed through the Limo as they swallowed their drinks. As they cruised through Miami, they were amazed at the beautiful real estate and cars people drove. Truth knew he would have to get his weight up to live good in Miami. Porches, Lambo's, Ferrari's, Bentley's, and

Benz's were as common as Cadillac's and box Chevy's were in Milwaukee.

"Do yawl see how they ridin' down hurr?" Trouble asked.

"I can't believe my damn eyes, they eating down here," Boss chipped in.

"Fuck the cars, I'm tryna go jet skiing," JaBar shouted out.

"And I'm tryna hit these boutiques up," Jazzie blurted as Raquel gave her a high five.

"We gone hit the Gucci Store tomorrow, babe, and blow a few thou'," Truth stated as he took a sip out of his wine flute.

"I'm with that!" Jazzie yelled out while doing a little dance in her seat.

As the Limo pulled in front of Braham's Auto, Truth felt like a kid in a candy store. They exited the Limo quickly. Everyone went their separate ways like they were in a trance lusting over the foreign cars. Boss' eyes were glued to a 1995 Mercedes Benz 600 SL, Trouble a 1993 Murcielago, JaBar a 1995 Lexus 470 SUV, Raquel and Jazzie a convertible Porsche 911, and Truth a convertible Dodge Viper.

A salesman spotted Truth staring hard at a Dodge Viper. Eager for a sale, he gained his composure then walked towards Truth.

"It has a supercharged V-10, 600 horsepower …"

Truth cut the salesman off in mid-sentence, "Brembo brakes, cool air intake, Burla exhaust."

The salesman was amazed at his education on the vehicle.

"Wow, I see you know a lot about this fine piece of machinery," the salesman stated with a smile.

"You can say that," Truth replied modestly as the salesman extended his hand.

"My name is Jim Van Horn," the salesman greeted.

"Truth," he replied.

"Nice to meet you, Truth," Jim said as the men shook hands.

"My attorney, Joel Fletcher, recommended me to you," Truth explained how he came upon the dealer.

"Ohhh, you're the friend he told me about. So what can I help you with?"

Dollar signs twinkled in Mr. Van Horn's eyes like diamonds.

"I had my eyes set on this Dodge Viper," he explained.

"I see you a person that knows what he likes and wants," Mr. Van horn noted with a smile.

"Oh yeah, I'm very persistent," Truth replied.

Mr. Van Horn knew the Dodge Viper only ran $60,000 and his commission off the sale would be decent, but he had his mind set on a bigger commission and he could get it by selling something more expensive. Mr. Van Horn led Truth over to a '94 Ferrari Testarossa. It belonged to a convicted drug lord from the Medellin Cartel, which made it hard to sell.

"Look at this beauty. This is top of line fine engineering, and it fits you better than the Dodge Viper. The Viper is cool, but it doesn't say you made it like this does. Plus, it's a convertible and only has 3,000 original miles. Tim Hardaway use to own this car." Mr. Van Horn was really laying it on thick.

I can picture myself whipping this bitch, Truth thought to himself.

"I still like the Viper, Jim," Truth replied, trying to act like he wasn't that interested in the Ferrari.

Jazzie came by to see what was going on.

"You gone get the Viper, baby?" Jazzie asked as she wrapped her arm around Truth's waist.

"I don't know. Me and Jim negotiating now."

Jazzie was confused. She wondered why Truth was standing in front of a Ferrari if he wanted a Viper.

"Truth, could you please step into my office?" Jim stated as he interrupted Jazzie.

"Sure," Truth replied with a confused look on his face.

"Ladies, would you please excuse us?" Mr. Van Horn requested as he led Truth towards his office then shut his door.

"Look Truth, if you purchase the Ferrari I'll give it to you for 130k, tax, title and registration included." Mr. Van Horn stared Truth directly into his eyes not blinking once.

Why he tryna sell this car so bad? Truth pondered. Fuck it, you only live once. Plus, I got 'bout three mill' stashed, this ain't putting a dent in my pockets. I can make this back off one flip, Truth reasoned.

"Let's do it, Jim."

"I knew you'd come to your senses. I'm practically giving you this car," Mr. Van Horn lied.

"Well, let me call Joel and have him take care of the paper work."

"Cool, you should be ready to pick it up tomorrow then." Mr. Van Horn said as he rose from his desk to give Truth a strong handshake, relieved he finally sold the hot Ferrari.

Chapter 9

The time was 11P.M, South Beach strip was starting to come alive. People were out in droves ready to get their party on. Jazzie and Raquel were dressed in form fitting Chanel skirts, Manolo Blahnik heels, and draped in enough jewelry to brighten up any room. Truth was geared from head to toe in Prada. He decided to go conservative with his jewelry game. He threw on a two carat diamond pinky ring and a Platinum Rolex.

Boss on the other hand, was Louis Vuitton'd up from head to toe. JaBar and Trouble went with some Gucci attire. Thick gold Herringbone necklaces with diamond encrusted Jesus medallions rested on their chest. Truth and his entourage didn't have a particular destination 'til they saw the big crowd standing outside of Club Rolexx.

"Driver pull over, we hitting this club up!" Truth yelled from the back of the limo.

As they exited the limo, people were staring hard wondering who they were.

"The V.I.P line over here!" The big burly Haitian bouncer announced. Truth and his squad walked over to the V.I.P line, they weren't trying to be standing outside all night while people partied inside. "How many with cha, bruh?" The bouncer asked.

"It's six of us," Truth replied as he turned around to do a re-count.

"That'll be $400," the bouncer stated.

Truth dug inside his pocket and peeled off five c-notes then handed them to the bouncer.

"Keep the change," Truth replied as he winked at the bouncer.

"Thanks mane," the bouncer shot back with a big smile.

Before entering the club the crew was pat searched, but not thoroughly since Truth gave the bouncer a $100 tip. As they stepped inside Club Rolexx, the smell of sweet perfumes lingered in the air along with the aroma of good weed smoke and men's colognes. Junior M.A.F.I.A. song "Get Money" was blasting in the background out of the 2000 watt sound system while the strippers worked the crowd after their stage sets. Some of the dancers were giving lap dances while others were making love in the club in the V.I.P. section.

Money was raining over the dancers. This was the first time Truth and his team witnessed anything like this. Truth couldn't understand why niggaz would just throw money away on strippers in large amounts. These some tricking ass niggaz, Truth thought to himself as he smirked at Boss.

Hoes were bussing it wide open on stage, leaving nothing to the imagination. Women were eating each other out and pulling niggaz from the crowd to join them. Truth, Trouble, JaBar, and Boss thought they were in heaven. This was a major upgrade from Tommy's and The Cheetah Club back in Milwaukee. They made their way to the V.I.P section then made themselves comfortable. A thick dark skinned waitress wearing a bra and thong approached their table to take their orders.

Truth couldn't understand why the waitress wasn't on stage. She was definitely eye candy with good earning potential. She stood 5'3", had a few tattoos, a flat stomach, and blonde hair cut short like Nia Long. When she spoke Truth couldn't put his finger on what her nationality was.

"What can I do for yawl?"

"Bring us six bottles of Cristal, it's my birthday," Truth flirted back, flashing his teeth.

Jazzie wasn't fond of Truth's actions, but she kept her mouth shut seeing that it was his birthday.

"Oh really?" The waitress replied with a smile.

"If you don't mind me asking, what's your nationality?" Jazzie asked while cutting her eyes at Truth.

"I'm Dominican and Black," the waitress disclosed as she placed her hand on her hips.

"Ohh, you're pretty," Jazzie complimented while admiring the waitress' beauty.

"Thanks," the waitress replied softly. "Well, let me go fill this order for yawl so yawl can start partying," the waitress insisted politely.

"You enjoying yo'self, Daddy?" Jazzie asked Truth.

"Yeah babe. It feels so good to be away from the city," Truth specified.

"I can second that!" Raquel shot back.

Shortly the waitress returned with the bottles of Cristal. Truth tipped her with a fifty dollar bill. Jazzie whispered something to the waitress, causing her to crack a smile. Five minutes later, the DJ made an announcement on the mic.

"I wanna say happy birthday to Truth! He came all the way from Milwaukee to celebrate with Club Rolexx! Truth, where you at! Bring yo' ass to the stage, we got a special surprise fo' you!"

Truth stared at his boys then smiled, then over at Jazzie.

"Go up there Daddy, see what they got planned for you," Jazzie insisted with a sneaky smile on her face.

Truth stood up slowly then headed up to the stage with a bottle of Cristal in his hand. One dancer grabbed his free hand and led him to a chair that sat behind a stripper pole. Truth had no idea what would happen next.

"You Remind Me" by R Kelly was playing in the background as four thick dancers strutted on stage then started gyrating in front of Truth. Truth loved all the ass and titties swagging in his face. He figured he would make it rain like the Miami niggaz was doing.

"Happy Birthday Truth! Welcome to Miami, ain't he a lucky muh fucka yawl!" The DJ yelled, causing the crowd to go wild.

Things started to heat up as the dancers poured chocolate syrup and whipped cream on each other, then licked it off. The crowd was in a frenzy. The act got wilder when the dancers pulled out dildos and started fucking each other with them.

Truth's snake was throbbing inside his pants. He wanted to strip out of his clothes and join the action. Instead, Truth poured Cristal over the dancers while they continued to play with their sex toys on stage. Everybody was staring at Jazzie in disbelief. They couldn't believe she allowedd Truth to go on stage. Jazzie just kept smiling, she knew her man was enjoying himself and that's

all that mattered to her. Plus, she knew he was gone fuck the hell out of her after being so aroused by the sexy dancers.

Jazzie had been drinking too much and started feeling herself. She rose from the table and walked on stage. Jazzie stood in front of Truth and stared at him seductively. She dropped to her knees and unzipped Truth pants. The dancers had confused looks on their face. Jazzie pulled Truth's dick out and inserted it inside her hot mouth. It only took Truth three minutes before he exploded. Truth was so excited by the night's events. He felt like a real hood star.

When the music stopped the crowd was clapping and chanting, "Truth! Truth! Truth!

Truth!"

While all this was going on Trouble and JaBar found themselves a dancer that was going and paid for some head. They were enjoying every moment of the Miami lifestyle. Truth's entourage drank enough liquor for a party of twelve. They were having so much fun when they looked up it was 4A.M. Truth managed to do a lil politicking with some major Miami niggaz in the V.I.P. section. They could see from a mile away Truth was getting money, and figured he could be an asset to them in the future.

Truth thought they were D-Boys, but in actuality they were CEO's of their record label.

"I see why you wanna move on to bigger and better thangs, Truth," Boss stated.

"Mane bruh, this is the life I want right hurr. I love the Mill, but we can't kick it like this thurr. Tomorrow I'll have my own Ferrari, the Feds would be at my ass back home fo' that purchase, bruh."

"Damn right they would, East," Boss agreed while nodding his head.

"That's why I gotta invest in Future and get some of this rap money, bruh."

"You really serious 'bout starting a label, huh?" Boss asked while grinning.

"Bruh, if you wanna be a part of this shit we can let Trouble run the show while we run the label. I mean, itz on you folks," Truth stated seriously.

"I don't know shit 'bout the music industry, Truth," Boss complained.

"Don't worry, I don't either, but who says we can't hire some people that do?"

Boss studied Truth wondering if he was ready for the next level of hustling. As they exited the club, Truth thanked DJ Rankin' for all the love he showed him. He decided to invite him to his all white birthday bash. The only stipulation was DJ Rankin' had to bring some of the ladies from the club with him.

****

"Milltown in da house, party over here!" Someone yelled from the pool area.

DJ Kaos' got the party crunk when he played the 2Pac song, "Gangsta Party." Everybody started throwing up their sets while vibing to the track.

"Happy Birthday to my homie, Truth! Milwaukee definitely in Miami showing out!" DJ Kaos' yelled over the microphone.

The catering service was a blend of imagination, expertise, and creativity. There was grilled shrimps and filet mignon, chicken breast with lime sauce, slow cooked barbeque ribs, and grilled Rock Lobster tails. There were an assortment of Southern side dishes such as, corn on the cob, Étouffée, mustard and collard greens, macaroni, jambalaya, hot water cornbread, and gumbo.

Truth spared no expense. He called on Divine Delicacies of Miami to create his birthday cake. The cake measurements were 60x 30, chocolate chip with chocolate fondant icing, with a picture of Truth's face showing his gold teeth with a cloud of hundred dollar bills floating around him.

****

The sky was clear and blue as the ocean water, the temperature was 88○ not a cloud in sight. People were playing volleyball topless, skinny dipping, snorting cocaine, and having sex wherever it was space. The pimps and playaz sat around the pool area politicking while sipping

$350 bottles of Don Perignon Rose Champagne. When Jazzie saw Heaven at the party she was infuriated. She bit down on her bottom lip while she watched her like a hawk.

"What this bitch doin' here?' Jazzie muttered.

Raquel saw the look of disgust on Jazzie's face and quickly reacted.

"Not today Bitch, this is Truth's day. We ain't came way down here to be beating bitches ass. We on vacation, fool." Raquel countered as she grabbed Jazzie's arm, leading her away from Heaven's presence.

Heaven's curvaceous body complimented the white Prada two piece she was wearing. She could've easily been mistaken for a model. Heaven mingled with everyone at the party. She was hoping she would bump into Truth. Unfortunately, he was too busy smoking weed with Future and the rest of the folks on the far end of the estate.

"Bruh, I like how you put this together. I want my birthday party to be this fly," Future implied.

"Shiiiidd bruh, when we get our label rollin' we gone be living like this ourselves," Truth professed as he blew out a cloud of thick weed smoke.

"Puff, puff, pass ugly ass nigga," Boss joked as he anxiously reached his hand out to receive the blunt.

"Hurr my nigga. Somebody fire up anotha blunt I'm tryna get high as the moon," Truth uttered slowly.

"Shiiidd cuz, I already did," Trouble replied in a slow drawl.

"Yawl get use to this shit hurr 'cause we gone be living like this if yawl handle yawl business and keep fuckin' with me," Truth assured his entourage.

Baby Drew's "Powder" CD was blasting in the background as the blunts continued to circulate. Seconds later the music stopped and feedback from the DJ's microphone rang out of the humongous speakers.

"Attention! Attention! Where the birthday man at! You been hiding all damn day, itz time to show yo' face nigga!" King Mitch yelled. The crowd started chanting, "Truth! Truth! Truth! Truth! Truth!"

Future stared at Truth then cracked a smile.

"You hear dat, bruh?"

"Yup," Truth grinned as he tried to conceal his happiness.

"They want you, bruh."

"I know."

"Itz time for you to join the rest of the party," Future stated, trying to geek Truth up.

"Letz roll yawl. Bruh, you suppose to be performing anyway, so let's rock this bitch."

"Act like it then."

Truth headed towards the stage area with his entourage. Wwhen DJ saw Future he started spinning his records.

"Welcome to the stage Milltown's own, Fuuuture!"

The crowd went wild screaming and whistling as Future approached the mic.

"Yawl ready to get it cracking in this bitch!!" Future yelled through the microphone. "I can't hear yawl! Are yawl ready to get it cracking in this mutha fucka!"

The crowd started chanting Future name, his adrenaline was pumping, he was ready to rock the stage. DJ Kaos' put on a stellar performance on the ones and twos as Future went into his set. Truth was on stage performing as Future's hype man. He didn't mind playing the back. He wanted his brother to get his proper shine. By the time Future went into his fourth song, the crowd was so geeked they started bum rushing the stage. No harm was done being that everyone knew each other at the party.

Heaven studied Truth while he was on stage admiring his swagger. If she didn't know any better, it looked like Future and Truth already performed together a million times from the way they fed off each other's energy. As Future's show was coming to an end, Jazzie rushed on stage and grabbed the mic.

"Yawl having a good time!"

"Yeaaahhhh!" The crowd responded back.

"I can't hear yawl! Yawl havin' fun tonite!"

"Yeaaaahhh!" The crowd roared back.

"Good! We have a lot of lovely people here, and we appreciate yawl traveling so far to celebrate Truth's Birthday. I love you baby!"

Truth began to blush. He tried his best to look cool, but the love he was receiving felt too good inside.

"I love you too Jazz," Truth replied.

He walked over to Jazzie and planted a kiss on her cheek. The crowd started whistling and cheering for the ghetto fabulous couple. Jazzie and Truth were the black version of Bonnie and Clyde. The only difference was Jazzie was playing the game raw. After their warm embrace, Jazzie reached inside her Coach bag and pulled out a diamond necklace that she had King Mitch the jeweler make.

"Happy Birthday Truth!" Jazzie said as she put the necklace around Truth's neck and kissed him.

Heaven couldn't bare watching Jazzie and Truth on stage kissing, the sight alone made her sick to her stomach. Truth smiled as he lifted the diamond necklace up to get a better look at it.

King Mitch grabbed the mic so he could say a few words. He knew Truth liked the piece he made from Truth's facial expression.

"Truth, remember I told you I had a surprise for you?" Truth nodded his head up and down. "Well, I present to you this I-94 piece, the first of its kind! I hope you didn't think you was gone be wearing a diamond necklace without a new piece!"

The crowd was stunned by the beauty of the red, white, and blue diamonds. Truth gazed at the piece in amazement as King Mitch put it on him.

"Thanks King Mitch, this piece killing shit!"

Truth turned around to face the crowd as camera lights flashed. This was truly a moment to remember for him. Truth's closet associates stepped on stage to take pictures with him, causing him to feel like a rapper that just finished performing at a big concert.

"Baby, let's cut the cake, I wanna taste it," Jazzie pouted.

"Hold up, I gotta holla at the dudes I met at the club last night," Truth replied.

"Okay, don't be all day baby."

"Don't trip shawty, I just wanna chop it up with them real quick."

Truth strutted over towards to the two businessmen with the swagger of a true mogul.

"Truth, you and Future tore it up on stage, who you signed to?" Blue asked.

"Nobody yet, we 'bout to start our own label."

"Really? That's whuz up. He's talented. Me and my partner already in the business. If you need any help getting your label off the ground we can help you get to the top."

"Thanks, I'll definitely keep that in mind."

"Yawl make sure yawl enjoy yaself, fam. Itz plenty liquor, food, and hoes running around this bitch."

"Aight Truth, thanks for inviting us to your party. I hope this is the beginning of a prosperous friendship."

"It just might be, bruh." Blue said as he handed Truth his business card and they shook hands.

On his way back to cut the cake, Heaven stopped Truth and handed him a birthday card. "Happy birthday handsome," she smiled.

"Thanks boo." Truth replied as he opened the card.

"I liked the show. This party was pretty wild, but I enjoyed myself."

Heaven kept fidgeting with her hair as Truth stared into her eyes, it was obvious she was nervous.

"Yeah, it was wild. Shiiidd, we had to do it big down hurr babay. I'm glad you had fun though."

"This setting reminds me of a rap video," Heaven pointed out.

"Heaven, I'm 'bout ready to make you my new wifey," Truth expressed seriously.

"You ain't ready, you still in love with Jazzie," Heaven shot back as she turned away from Truth.

She wanted to believe Truth, but her heart wouldn't allow it.

"Jazzie been real foul lately, I'm just waiting for the right time to dump her ass," Truth confessed while shaking his head.

Heaven turned back around to face Truth.

"That sucks. I hope whatever problems yawl having yawl can work them out," Heaven proclaimed, even though she didn't mean a word she said; she actually was happy to hear they were having relationship issues.

"Heaven, she been lying 'bout her where abouts, thatz one thang I don't condone. Once you tell one lie, you gotta tell a million more, ya dig?"

"That's so true. Well, I'm 'bout to go holla at Reggie Brown and DJ Thrax."

"Okay, I'm 'bout to cut my cake. Don't give nobody none of my pussy," Truth insinuated with a grin.

Heaven placed her hand on her hip as she rolled her eyes at Truth.

"Until you drop yo' bitch, I think this kitty kat belongs to me." Heaven blew Truth a kiss then slowly walked away. She stopped after walking a few steps then slowly spun around facing Truth. "By the way nice car, hope you not foolish enough to bring it back to Milwaukee," Heaven stated while looking Truth up and down.

"Don't worry, I'm on top of minez," Truth emphasized.

Truth parked his Ferrari next to the stage so everyone could get a glimpse of it. If he could've put it on stage he would have. As he walked over to cut his cake, Truth thought about how Heaven would look on his arm, but the sight of Jazzie snapped him back to reality. I gotta 86 this bitch when we get back, but how? Truth pondered.

"Here come my big bruh, come on nigga cut this cake. I want a big piece!" Future uttered excitedly.

"Hold yo' horses bruh, you gone get a piece," Truth replied with a big smile.

Before Truth could dig into the cake, everyone started singing "Happy Birthday" to him. Truth was definitely embarrassed, Future even added two candles on the cake with the numbers 2 – 3 on it.

When they were done singing Boss walked over to Truth and whispered, "Blow out the candles and make a wish, nigga."

Truth blew out the candles and made his wish. He wished that by next year he would be out of the game, with Heaven, and in the music industry. Truth fed Jazzie some cake. She thought that was so sweet of him, and suddenly her conscious started to get the best of her. She wasn't sure what direction their future was going in, but she put all the drama to the side for the sake of making sure Truth enjoyed his day.

Heaven was eyeing Jazzie from afar wondering, How did she even get in the position to become his woman? She faker than a three dollar bill. Heaven decided to approach Truth in front of Jazzie, just to see how she would react. Heaven put on the sexiest walk she could muster up. Future licked his lips as he lusted after Heaven, wondering what the beautiful eye candy taste like.

"Excuse me Truth, can you tell me where the bathroom is?" Heaven inquired seductively.

Jazzie's face instantly frowned up. She couldn't believe the nerve of Heaven.

"Don't you see me and my man having a moment to ourselves?" Jazzie stated coldly.

"Please excuse her, its one upstairs in the master bed room to your left," Truth replied calmly.

"Thanks Truth," Heaven retorted with a smurk.

Oh no this Bitch didn't just flirt with my man in my face. Truth act like he diggin' this Bitch too, Jazzie thought to herself. Heaven got the reaction she was looking for and couldn't stop smiling as she walked away. After seeing Heaven again Truth was sexually aroused, and he needed to release some tension. Boss and Future told Truth they had a special surprise waiting on him in the theater room. Truth was curious as to what the surprise could be, so he excused himself from Jazzie's presence.

Once Truth was out of Jazzie's presence, he rushed over to the theater. When he opened the door his eyes were instantly bucked. A porno was playing on the wide screen while a live orgy was taking place. Boss and Future arranged for Truth to get some head by four women, all of different ethnic backgrounds. Truth took a seat next to Future as he grinned.

"Bruh, we got the door, enjoy these beautiful women, this one on us."

Future rushed to the door and locked it while the four women slowly got undressed. When they came out of their pants Truth's snake was standing at attention. The ladies all started sucking and nibbling on Truth like Piranhas. They kept his snake in rotation sucking on it. Whoever didn't have it in their mouth was either licking on his chest or balls. Truth had the biggest smile planted on his face as he fingered the women's wet juice boxes. The only sounds that could be heard in the room was slobbing and moaning.

"Come on baby, give us that sweet cum all over my face," one of the women begged.

The head Truth was getting felt so good he started fucking the jump-off mouth like he was inside her hot juice box. While Truth was getting the best head he had in a long time the other two women were on the side of him eating each other out. The sight alone almost made Truth bust a nut.

"Ohh! I'm finna cum!" Truth shouted as his body began to jerk uncontrollably.

The ladies held their tongues out with their eyes closed as Truth shot his warm load all over their sweaty faces. One of the ladies felt like she didn't get enough cum, so she started sucking Truth's snake, trying to get the last drop. Future sensed they were done so he walked over to Truth and handed him a towel.

"You straight, bruh?" Future asked with a smirk on his face.

"Yeah mane, thanks fo' da present, nigga," Truth replied as he tried to catch his breath.

"Anythang fo' my big bruh. I see Boss over there getting it in, ha ha!"

"He sho is, ha ha!" Truth affirmed as he pulled his pants up.

"Bruh, who was ol' girl you was talkin' to earlier?" Future asked.

"Oh, that's da bitch, Heaven."

"She a bad bitch, bruh!" Future declared excitedly.

"She'll soon be taking Jazzie spot, bruh," Truth assured Future.

"What! Bruh, Jazzie gone snap!"

"I don't give a fuck," Truth stated in his best Bernie Mac impression as he explained why Jazzie was threading on thin ice with him.

Future was shocked by what Truth told him. He admired Jazzie. He knew his big brother didn't get emotionally attached that easy to women, so if he introduced her to him he knew he had a lot of feeling for her.

"I'm sorry to hear that, bruh. What you gone do now?" Future inquired.

Truth inhaled then exhaled, "Itz not important now. We on vacation. Bruh, last night I met some record execs at the booty club. They left me their business card too, so I invited them to the party and had a lil convo with them." He stated.

"You know this industry shady, don't start trusting shit people say. This shit like the dope game," Future stated.

"I heard Master P say that too, bruh," Truth replied.

"Now why you think he said that, Truth? He ain't say that just to be saying it." Future explained.

Truth let what Future just explained to him sink in his head and took heed. He knew the dope game, and Future knew music.

"Bruh, can you put my Ferrari in storage for me? I want to keep it in Atlanta. I can't take this hot muh fucka back to the Mill."

"Good! I was sho' starting to worry 'bout yo' fool ass for a sec."

"I just wanna stomp with the big dogs when I'm in town so we can get in the door faster. Shiiidd, you gotta look like money to attract money," Truth testified.

Future nodded his head in agreement. After being in Atlanta for a year, he figured out fast that people judged you off your material possessions. Truth's party was a huge success. It wasn't one incident, therefore the police didn't have to show up. The streets respected Truth greatly so they knew they'd have to pay for coming down to Miami fucking up his party.

"I'm gone have to pay a nice piece of change to clean this bitch up," Truth pondered as he gazed over the estate.

"Bruh, we need to come up with a name fo' our label," Future suggested.

"Ummm, how 'bout DBoyz ENT.?"

Future stared at Truth wondering if was he out of his mind.

"Nah bruh, ah ah, we need something different than that,"
Future stated as he gazed at Truth's I-94 piece.

"I got it," Future mumbled to himself. "I-94 ENT, bruh!" Future shouted.

"Huh!" Truth responded confused. "That's it, I-94 ENT! And you already got the piece made, bruh. All you need to do is get King Mitch to make me one so I can rep in Atlanta," Future was ecstatic.

"Thatz brilliant bruh. We'll be like Death Row with our pieces," Truth stated proudly.

"Yup I-94 ENT, datz what it is, Truth," Future agreed as he grinned.

It was 3AM, people were still partying. The heavy cocaine usage had the party going in full throttle. Truth, Jazzie, Boss, Raquel, Future and a lady he met at the party all went down to the small lake on the estate to relax and catch a breeze.

"Nice piece Truth, King Mitch sprayed that bitch up," Raquel stated as she lifted the medallion up and examined it.

"Thank you Raquel, Mitch over did it this time. This muh fucka need to be insured," Truth insisted as he gazed at his I-94 ENT medallion.

"Isn't this beautiful yawl?" Boss asked as he absorbed the beautiful scenery.

"I'm in love with this mansion, and we only been here for a second. The money good back home, but I ain't in a rush to go back, yawl. Being hurr gives me peace of mind. I don't feel that in Milwaukee. I think I'm 'bout to turn over a new leaf and give the game up."

Boss let out a loud burp, "Excuse me yawl, drank too much champagne."

Everyone was tipsy and feeling themselves so they didn't take Truth serious.

"Boy shut up, you know you can't leave the streets alone, the fuck else you gone do?" Raquel stated jokingly.

Boss grabbed Raquel then gave her a sloppy kiss. Boss and Raquel were so into each other as they kissed passionately and fondled one another. Moments later they were tugging at each other's clothes ready to set it off then and there.

"Ahhh, look at them Truth, they're so cute," Jazzie whispered while admiring the way Boss held Raquel close to his body.

"I'll show you what's cute," Truth shot back as he picked Jazzie up and carried her to a quiet spot.

Truth sat Jazzie down and told her to stare up at the sky. He slid Jazzie panties off then started licking on her swollen clitoris. As the fresh air from the lake grazed Jazzies skin, it sent an invigorating sensation over her tense body. Jazzie couldn't sit still. Her body squirmed like a fish on dry land as Truth's tongue worked wonders. Truth knew her hot spots, so he used it to his advantage as Jazzie moaned in ecstasy.

"Baby, you make me feel so good," Jazzie moaned softly as she stared up at the sky.

She started thinking about her past, present, and future, realizing this was the first time in her life she ever been loved so hard. Law didn't shower Jazzie with the same amount of affection Truth did, but she was in debt to Law and mentally he had a hold on her. Tears of guilt trickled down her face as Truth's tongue caressed her throbbing pearl tongue. As Jazzie reached her orgasm, her body shook violently causing her back to arch up. Truth stood up then entered Jazzie's soaking wet juice box, inserting every inch of his swollen snake inside of her.

Jazzie bit on her lip as Truth planted his hands on the grass and positioned himself in a push up position. Jazzie loved when Truth got in this position because he was able to get deeper inside of her. Jazzie reached her climax again. Truth felt himself about to cum, and Jazzie could also tell by the way his body tensed up. She pushed him off of her and caught all his warm juices, sucking Truth bone dry.

Truth was completely drained as he flopped over and fell asleep on Jazzie's chest. She exhaled slowly as she caressed his back. This was very soothing to her, ultimately causing her to fall asleep. As the sun slowly rose the hot rays beamed over their naked bodies, causing Truth and Jazzie to wake up. Truth couldn't believe they fell asleep outside. As Truth rubbed the sleep out of his tired eyes, he nudged Jazzie.

"Ughhh, stop boy," Jazzie moaned groggily.

"Get up gurl, itz time to get up. You know we gone be leaving soon," Truth whispered.

"Ughh, I don't wanna go yet," Jazzie whined.

Truth smacked Jazzie on her plump ass cheeks.

"Get yo' spoiled ass up and call a cleaning service so we can get this place back in order," Truth commanded with a smile.

Jazzie rubbed her eyes; the sun almost blinded her.

"Damn Boss Man," Jazzie shot back as she reached for her clothes.

"You damn right," Truth stated as he kissed Jazzie on her dry lips.

"Baby, last night was beautiful, I never felt like that in my life," Jazzie confessed as she waited for Truth to respond.

"I'm glad you enjoyed it cuz as long as you keep it trill with me you'll always get treated like a Queen," Truth lied with a straight face.

Truth's words immediately made Jazzie feel guilty, but she still managed to crack a smile.

"We going jet skiing before we leave, baby?"

"Of course, we can't leave hurr without jet skiing. We ain't come this far not to hit the water."

****

While everyone was out on the Jet Ski's, Truth managed to have a minute with Heaven. He promised her he'd make time for her once they made it back to Milwaukee.

Future called a storage company in Atlanta that had twenty-four hour security so when the Ferrari made it to Atlanta it would have somewhere to be sheltered. Truth and Future decided to chill on the sand while everybody else played in the water like kids.

"Bruh, I was thinking we gone need a building for us to set up shop and look professional. You think you can shop around for a vacant building when you get back?"

"Yeah, I can do that. Make sure you be careful in the Mill, I ain't tryna put the ski mask and black gloves back on, nigga," Future stated seriously.

Truth cracked a smile, he knew Future wasn't playing.

"I'm good bruh, I try not to do that many transactions. That's what Boss and Trouble and dem fo'."

"I know bruh, but that don't mean you can't be touched. After today you gone be the talk of the city. How many niggaz can through a party like this from the Mill?"

Truth leaned his head to the side as he scratched his head, "Nobody bruh."

"I know, so watch yo' every step when you get back, bruh. Niggaz talk like bitches so please stay under the radar."

"Huh bruh, I just don't want to leave my folks behind."

"Worrying 'bout people gone get you killed, bruh. Think rationally bruh, if you wanna survive in this industry you gotta develop a shark's mentality." Truth couldn't believe the knowledge his lil brother just dropped on him, but he didn't ignore a word he said, he soaked it all in. "Truth watch out!" Future yelled as Boss made his Jet Ski splash a puddle of water on them.

"I'm fuckin' you up Boss!" Truth yelled as he looked down at his wet clothes.

"Think about what I just said to ya, big bruh."

"I will bruh, we gone make history together, believe dat."

Chapter 10

Black D was left in charge of Trouble's traphouse while they were out of town. While the crew was gone, Black D wasn't conducting business the way he was instructed to. He was totally reckless. He had girls over, skipping school and running trains on them with his niggaz, which was a major violation. The hood knew Trouble and JaBar were gone out of town, and the goons had never seen Black D before and wasn't feeling him getting money in the hood.

"That nigga in there slipping, East," Kwony stated.

"I know East, nigga must think itz sweet over here," Torry replied as he cracked his knuckles.

"Letz tear this nigga off then, this nigga reckless," Kwony suggested.

"What about Trouble and JaBar though, East?' Torry reasoned.

"They won't know who did it nigga, especially behind black ski masks," Kwony uttered as a grin slowly formed on his face.

"Fuck it then East, letz do this shit then."

The goons sent a crack head to the door to buy a sack. One of the young hood rats answered the door nonchantly, not paying any attention. One of the goons snatched the young girl up and placed the steel to her head, slowly leading her back inside. Black D got caught slipping. He wanted to reach for his piece, but it was too late.

"Fuck!"

"Don't even thank about it bruh, let me get that strap up out cha," the goon commanded as he snatched the pistol from Black D then whacked him over the head with it sending Black D face first to the floor.

The goons laid the whole house down, ransacking the house 'til they found the money and dope. They retrieved $1500 and four zips of cocaine.

"Where da rest of the shit! I know yawl holding in this bitch!" The Kwony yelled.

"Yawl got it all, nigga!" Black D barked back.

"You lucky I believe you, nigga. This wasn't suppose to happen this easy, nigga. I suggest next time you send a shooter to the door. This was a "just because" robbery, "just because" yo' ass was in our hood hustling reckless. We had to take a look at cha," Torry professed.

Black D hocked up a luggy and spit on Kwony's feet.

Kwony knelt down and whispered into Black D's ear, "I should push yo' wig back fo' doing that ho ass shit, but I don't wanna make it easy for you. You gone be in more trouble when Trouble and JaBar get back. I'ma let them deal with yo' stupid ass."

Kwony let off a round into the ceiling, causing Black D to jump then vanished into thin air. Black D knew he fucked up and didn't have an excuse for letting anybody rob the trap house; after all he was a certified goon himself.

****

Detective Bryant received a phone call from his old friend Captain Swartz. He was just informed that he was a possible suspect in a homicide, and there was someone willing to testify against him.

"What you get yourself into now, Bryant!" Captain Swartz yelled as he slammed his hand on his oak desk.

"Whoever your witness is, is full of shit! Tell me who the witness is!" Detective Bryant yelled as he punched the wall, knocking a chunk of drywall to the floor.

"You know I can't give you that information or my ass will be on the line. Well, you're gonna have to come down for questioning. After that we'll release you, I promise you. I'm sending a car over to pick you up," Captain Swartz stated.

Detective Bryant knew this trick too well. He knew once he was in custody, he would never see the light of day again.

"Don't send a car, I'll be down," he replied.

"Don't keep me waiting Bryant, cuz if you bullshit me I'm personally gone bust your balls!" Captain Swartz snapped as he slammed his phone down.

Captain Swartz' nerves were so bad he popped a few aspirins inside his mouth to calm himself down.

"I'm getting too old for this shit, I swear," he complained

Detective Bryant couldn't believe the turn of events happening in his life. He got caught having sex with a crack head and tossed in his own squad car trunk, he got suspended indefinitely without pay, his wife wanted a divorce, and to top it all off he just received the worst news he could possibly get. He knew Internal Affairs would be all over this case. Detective Bryant needed to figure out a plan and fast.

****

Boss hit the streets with a vengeance. After seeing how people lived in Miami, he realized his pockets weren't as fat as he thought they were. He had plans of taking over the Northside once Truth left the game. Boss knew going legit was out the question for him, he loved the allure of fast money too much. Knowing he was needed by D boys and crack heads made Boss feel important and gave him an adrenaline rush. In his mind he was making love to the money like a sex tape. The streets was his bitch, and he was in love with her. Boss was ready to touch his first million and become a shot caller, but he needed the plug Truth had.

Boss was in traffic rolling in his '95 Lexus GS400 bangin' "5 on It" by the Luniz. He decided to go ride down on Chub to try to get him on his line. Chub was a nigga that copped between three or four bricks. Boss rode through Chub's hood known as "The Ghetto," searching for him. He spotted Chub shooting dice in front of an abandoned house.

Boss rolled up and hit his horn a few times, BMMM, BMM, BM, BMMM! Chub scrunched his face as he studied the car. He had no idea who was behind the dark tint.

"Yo' roll Chub," one of the gamblers stated.

"Hold up, who dat!" Chub yelled while clutching on his waist.

Boss hit the button on his door panel, as his window slowly slid down he yelled, "Itz Boss nigga! Come holla at cha boy!"

Chub snatched his money up and pulled his pants up.

"Let me see what this nigga on," Chub stated.

"Damn fam, you just gone snatch yo' money out the pot?" One man questioned.

"Yup nigga," Chub confirmed as he raised his shirt up revealing his Glock 40.

"Aight Fam, I was just saying nigga, you ain't gotta show us yo' strap," the angry goon stated.

"I'll be right back, bitch ass nigga." Chub grilled.

As Chub approached Boss he wondered what he was on, it was odd of him to be on his side of town.

"Nigga, what you doing in The Ghetto Eastside ass nigga?"

"I'm here on business, fam. I got a nice proposition for yo' fat ass," Boss joked.

"Really? Let me hear this shit, this better be good," Chub responded.

"Yeah my nig, get in."

Chub stared at Boss for a second then hopped inside.

"Let me tell my niggaz I'll be back, Boss," Chub replied.

"No prob," Boss told stated.

"Say fam, I'll be back! Yawl better still be out here too. I'm tryna win some of my money back!" Chub yelled to the group of men.

"I see you running nigga, scared to lose that paper!" Another man joked back.

"Ha Ha! I'll be back, on my momma." Chub laughed. Boss smashed off fast, burning rubber. "I see you riding Foreign, nigga," Chub looked around the car.

"This? This ain't nothing, I'm tryna ride Lambo, my nigga," Boss professed, causing Chub to laugh.

"Yo' ass gone be in the Fedz facing the Rico Act, fool azz nigga."

Boss stared at Chub and grinned.

"Oh, I got a hungry lawyer who stay ready, believe that," Boss made known.

"Okay Nino," Chub shot back while shaking his head.

"Nah nigga, fuck Nino bitch ass, remember he turned out to be a snitch in the end, fuck dat nigga," Boss grilled.

"You right fam, so whatz da deal?"

Boss rubbed his goatee then grinned.

"Okay Chub, let me ask you something personal," Boss stated.

"Shoot."

It took a moment for him to gather his thoughts.

"How much you paying fo' yo' bricks?" Boss inquired.

"Twenty-nine, why?"

Boss' face lit up after hearing those numbers.

"I can give 'em to you fo' twenty-seven and a half if you fuck with me and only me."

"We never did business before, why you tryna fuck with me now?" Chub asked suspiciously.

Boss was getting irritated by Chub questioning him, so he made a hard right turn onto 20th N Lisbon then slammed on the brakes.

"Look fam, I got a plug, and I need a certified nigga to help me dump this shit! Now you can fuck with me and save some money or keep getting dicked, but I guarantee yo' shit ain't A1 like minez!" Boss snapped as he stared into Chub's eyes.

"Say homie, I hear what you saying and all, but the only problem is my peeps be throwing me whatever I buy and he gone wonder why I stopped fucking with him."

"Fuck that nigga, he'll get over it. I'll do the same for you. I'll toss you whatever you buy. I ain't with none of that fuck shit, nigga, tryna flip my money a few times before he hit my hand though."

"Fam, you ain't gotta come at me like that, I'm certified nigga," Chub barked aggressively.

"So we got a deal, fat ass nigga?" Boss asked then cracked a smile to lighten up the mood.

"Yeah nigga, and chill with that fat shit," Chub fired back.

Chub hated being teased about his weight because he heard every fat joke there was growing up. Boss dropped Chub off then focused on his next business partner, J Melo. As he cruised down 35th, the Lexus was turning heads left and right. The 18 inch chrome Blades were chopping like blenders, and niggaz weren't used to seeing big rims on cars yet.

As Boss took puffs off the blunt, he envisioned himself being on top of the world and people hanging on his nuts instead of Truth's. After seeing Truth cop a Ferrari, Boss became jealous hearted. Boss had no idea how much money Truth had, but the Ferrari definitely let him know they were in two different leagues.

"Oh there go J Melo," Boss mumbled as he pulled up across the street from the Ritz Fish Market and blew his horn.

"What up G?" Melo questioned.

"Tryna fuck with you, I got them numbers too, Melo."

"Oh, I'm good now Boss."

"Don't trip, what you paying?"

Boss already knew the answer to that question.

"I'm paying twenty-nine."

"Ewww, I got em for twenty-seven and a half and flake too."

"Fo' real?"

"Yup, and it's jumping back good, take my number down and holla at me once you dump that shit you got."

"Okay G, I got it locked in. When you cop that bitch?" J Melo asked, referring to Boss' Lexus.

"Oh, I copped this last year, you like it?"

"Yeah, how you fit them big ass rims on that bitch?" Melo inquired as Boss grinned.

"You gotta pay fo shit you want, folks," Boss bragged as he gave Melo some dap.

"Make sho' you fuck with a nigga though, I gotta keep it movin', J Melo," Boss stated as he gazed at his watch.

"Aight, I'm gone get up with cha, don't forget the price you gave me too, nigga."

"I'm a man of my word, fam, act like it fam no bullshit get at me."

When Boss hopped back inside his whip he thought, I'm 'bout to flood the streets and have the city on lock.

****

Joel Fletcher was looking over some files he had sitting on his desk when his phone started to ring. Who could this be? Joel Fletcher wondered as he took his glasses off and placed them on his desk.

"Hey buddy, it's Truth."

"Hey! Truth! You back already?"

"Yup, by the way, good looking out with errthang too."

"Is the mansion still in one piece?" Joel asked jokingly.

Truth started laughing, "Come on Joel, I wouldn't disrespect you like that," Truth made known.

"Good, now that we got that out the way, how can I help you?" Joel questioned.

"I want to start a record label. What you know about the business?"

Joel placed his index finger on his chin and exhaled.

"I know a little, but it's not my area of interest."

"Can you recommend anyone then?"

"Well, I can check around, but if you're serious I can study up on it and be your legal advisor."

"Cool, I don't want to deal with anyone else but you, Joel. Oh, I got a Mill ticket I need washed. I'm gone use it as seed money for my new business venture."

Joel grinned as he rubbed his chin. He now knew Truth was bigger than he portrayed himself to be.

"Aight, let me check with my investors to see how what we can do, come by my office tomorrow and we'll take it from there."

"Aight Joel, see you then."

"Where's the Ferrari?" Joel inquired seriously.

"Don't worry, I left it in Atlanta."

"Good, you already know I was about to question you about that, huh?"

"Yup."

"Well, I'm busy doing paper work Truth, call me tomorrow."

Joel Fletcher hung up the phone then shook his head, This cock sucker has a million dollars in cold hard cash, fucking unbelievable.

****

Trouble was heated when he got wind of what happened while they were gone. Black D had no idea who had robbed him, so retaliation was a problem. Since Trouble couldn't take his anger out on the robbers, he snapped and put hands on Black D like he was a total stranger, then put him on ice for a week.

Trouble regained order of his trap house and put a few extra soldiers on deck so the robbers wouldn't think it was sweet and double back. Trouble turnt his grind up to the max. He flew through a brick in a week, all in ten's, twenty's, 8Balls, and zips. After seeing how Miami niggaz were living, Trouble had a different outlook on what having money really was. He vowed that he was going back to Miami to cop something Foreign from Braman Auto by the summer.

****

The prices for bricks of cocaine never went back down in Milwaukee. Word on the street was a U-Haul truck was pulled over with four hunderd Kilo's stashed inside in Lake County, Illinois. A bust of this caliber definitely made things difficult in the streets of Milwaukee, seeing that the majority of the dope came from dealers from Chicago, Illinois. Fortunately, Truth had a California plug, so dope consistently flowed like water for him, and he was able to make a larger profit without having to bust his bricks down.

Truth's operation was running like a fine tuned machine, and that's the way he expected it to stay. Since Truth copped the Ferrari, he figured it was time for the whole squad to step their car game up. Joel Flethcer knew a foreign car dealer in Chicago that they could shop with that didn't do any background checks, as long as you had cash they made sure you was pulling off in your car of choice.

Boss copped a burnt orange 1994 Cadillac Alante, Truth a 1996 Acura Legend, Trouble a black 5 series BMW, Black D a 1995 Cadillac STS, Andre a Lexus SC 300, JaBar a 1995 Infiniti Q45, and Jazzie a Lexus SC400. The cars were all registered to a bogus rental car business so the Feds couldn't back track the cars to any of them and hit them with tax evasion.

Trouble and JaBar even paid a visit to King Mitch the jeweler and had him make them I-10 pieces so they could rep Louisiana. Truth had I-94 pieces made for the rest of his squad so they could start promoting the movement. The money they spent didn't put a dent in their pockets because Truth made sure they all were stacking and moved up each time they copped their dope. The first of the month was around the corner, so all the money they blew would be recouped, plus more.

After meeting with Joel Fletcher, Truth was told that the label would be a go. Truth also was informed on who all was snitching in the city. Chub's name came up, but he payed it no mind being that he didn't deal with Chub on any level.

"Thanks for putting me up on game, Joel."

"Ain't that what you pay me big bucks for, Truth?"

"You damn right, you taxing my ass too," Truth joked.

"Well, now that you know what's going on in the streets, take heed and continue to play the back because I don't want nothing happening to you."

"Joel, you worry too much, I'm a block bleeda. I know how to handle myself in the streets."

"Okay well, call me later, maybe we can do lunch."

"Sounds like a plan."

****

Mileena was the backbone of Truth's operation, and to commemorate her for her loyalty Truth presented her with an I-94 piece and chain and a gold 1995 Lexus ES 300. With the amount of dope niggaz copped on the Northside and what Mileena moved on the Southside, Truth would need a bigger shipment of cocaine. He made sure he took good care of Mileena because she was always there with him when it was time to hit the kitchen and do the cooking.

****

Bzzz, Bzzzz, Bzzzz, Bzzzz, was the sound of Detective Bryant's cell phone.

"Hello?"

"Hello Detective Bryant, Dianne from forensics."

"Oh, hi Dianne. How can I help you?"

"I'm not supposed to be giving you this information, but we found some pubic hair on your friend Rudy that didn't belong to him."

Detective Bryant was at full attention at the mention of his deceased friend, Rudy.

"Then who does it belong to?" Detective Bryant inquired.

"To a Ms. Jasmine Jones."

Detective Bryant's blood began to boil as he balled his fist.

"That dirty bitch!"

"Well, I have to go, keep this between us."

"I sure will, and thanks again Dianne."

"No wonder I been sweating her, my spidey senses led me to Ms. Jasmine for a reason. This bitch gone have to pay for whatever part she played in Rudy's death. Fuck, I got that murder charge hanging over my head. How am I gone get out of that? Shit! When it rains it pours."

****

Heaven looked at her car then shook her head, "Damn, I need a car wash."

Somebody scribbled "Please wash me" on the driver door, Heaven noticed it after she was done doing a property showing. I can stop by Truth's car wash and get a free wash, plus I might bump into him, Heaven thought as she headed towards the car wash.

Heaven pulled into the parking lot. She noticed a candy blue Acura Legend parked all by itself gleaming in the sun. She knew it was Truth's whip, the car definitely fit his swag. Heaven suddenly became nervous as goose bumps surfaced on her flawless skin.

"What kind of wash do you want, Lil Momma?" Asked one of the workers.

"Give me the deluxe wash. Hold up, is Truth here?" Heaven asked, trying to make sure the Acura was his.

"Yup," the worker replied while squinting at Heaven.

"Well, he owes me a free wash. Can you tell him Heaven here so you won't get in any trouble?"

"Sure, you said Heaven right?"

"Yup."

The worker went to talk to Truth to confirm what Heaven just said. He didn't want his pay getting cut because a cute face pulled a fast one on him. Truth was on the phone caking with Jazzie when he heard a knock on the door.

"Come in."

"Truth, some lady name Heaven out front said she could get a deluxe wash on the house, I didn't do it though. I figured I'd holla at you first."

"Ha, Ha, I'll be out thurr in a sec, bruh."

"Okay."

"You better be home when I get thurr, Jazzie."

"I will be Truth, where else am I gone be?"

Truth didn't respond, he just closed his flip on his cell phone then headed towards the waiting area where Heaven was posted.

"So what brings you hurr?" Truth asked with a wide grin on his face.

"Obviously my car is dirty, and I heard y'all were the best in town," Heaven lied.

"Oh really?" Truth laughed.

He knew she was there to really see him.

"Yes really," she stated bashfully.

"You know I missed you, Heaven," Truth confessed.

Heaven was caught off guard so she took a moment to respond.

"I missed you too. What's going on with your situation?" She questioned.

"It's still complicated. When I get rid of her I don't want no strings attached so you can have me all to yo'self." Truth let her know.

Heaven couldn't keep herself from blushing. She felt like she was the luckiest woman in the world. She set out to get something, and she had actually gotten it. It was a feeling of bliss.

"I feel ya Truth. Other than that, how's business?"

"I'm starting a record label with my brother next year. I just had a meeting with my lawyer," Truth explained.

"That sounds like a good idea. I got a cousin that has a degree in marketing. If you need help in that area I could introduce you to her," Heaven implied.

"Damn Heaven, you plugged all around the board. I need you on my team. Jazzie's a liability, all she does is help spend my money," Truth complained.

Heaven laughed, she couldn't be mad at Jazzie for spending Truth's money. After all, what else was it for?

"Truth, that's what you get for trusting a big butt and smile. You gotta go for brains too," Heaven specified referring to herself.

"I'm gone need to sell the salon once I move to Atlanta to start my label."

Heaven did a double take. She thought she was hearing things. He's really serious about this label shit, and thinking of moving to Atlanta, Heaven thought to herself.

"Don't you have somebody in your family that can run the salon?" Heaven asked.

Truth thought to himself for a moment. He didn't want to lose one of his businesses.

"Matter fact I do," Truth replied as he rubbed his chin. Aunt Lucille can run the salon, Truth thought to himself. "What you got up fo' today?" Truth inquired as he caressed Heaven's hand.

"I gotta head back to the office to finish up some paper work on this house I just closed on, why?" Heaven inquired, while thumbing through her palm pilot.

"Because I'm 'bout to take you to Red Lobster. You feel like driving to Brookfield?" He questioned.

Heaven stared at Truth then let out a deep sigh, "Come on boy, I'll drive."

Truth and Heaven didn't order any food. They had a few drinks and took the time to really get to know each other. They realized they both had similar goals in life. Heaven found out that Truth wasn't shallow as your typical everyday hustla. Truth delved into his childhood, touching on how he lost his mother at a young age and having to fend for himself. Heaven felt compassion for Truth.

Truth asked Heaven why she was single. She explained that she hasn't met anyone that can think outside the box, and that all niggaz wanted to do was fuck her. Heaven was far from a hood rat. She had class about herself and wasn't going to settle for less when she had so much to offer.

"Look Truth, it's getting late, I enjoyed this meeting."

"Meeting? You mean date!"

"No, this wasn't a date. I gotta get back to the office now."

"I do too. Wow, you cold."

Heaven leaned in towards Truth and planted a warm kiss on his cheek. Truth was perplexed. He couldn't understand why Heaven was playing so hard to get. One thing for sure, he wasn't about to give up, he was determined to make Heaven his wifey. When they made it back to the wash Truth took Heaven's hand and gently kissed it. What a gentleman, Heaven thought.

"Have a good day Heaven, I enjoyed your company."

"Okay Truth, oh by the way, I enjoyed myself too." Heaven was smiling as she drove off to her office. "His nose wide open for me. Jazzie, you 'bout to loose yo' man." She said to herself.

Federal Agent McGee was sitting in his squad car sipping on a cup of Cafe Americano reading the Milwaukee Journal metro section. He was waiting for one of his informants to pull up so he could inform him on what was happening in the streets.

"So what you got for me, Chub?" Agent McGee asked.

"I told you I'll call you once I got something, man! Stop sweating me!" Chub barked aggressively.

"Don't forget who the fuck you work for, you lousy piece of shit! You the one that got knocked with two kilo's and an AK-47, bitch ass nigga! So get yo' fat ass out there and bring me somebody! I don't care if you gotta snitch on yo' grandmother!" Agent McGee frowned, lifting his face up as he flicked his cigarette butt in Chub's face.

Chub hated the position he was in, but it was either he do time or snitch. So far nobody had an idea he was working with the Fedz, but what's done in the dark comes to light. Chub thought about the conversation he had with Boss earlier. I can't do Boss in, he's a certified head bussa. I gotta get somebody that don't pose a threat but who?

Chub was out on the Federal bracelet for a year and had put in work in other cities. He was about to go platinum from snitching, which is nothing to be proud of on the streets.

"Bingo!" Chub whispered to himself.

He remembered that he had some vital information on a robbery/ homicide one of his worker's cousins did, so he decided to fork that info over to Agent McGee. Chub told Agent McGee everything he knew about the crime plus some stuff Agent McGee didn't care to know. Chub was trying his best to keep himself on the streets with his baby momma and kids. What he didn't know was he still wasn't off the hook yet. When the Fedz needed him again he would have to produce, or they'd threaten to lock his ass up and charge him with his original case.

****

"The First of the Month" by Bone Thugs and Harmony was playing in the background as Truth made his rounds. It was actually the first of the month, and people were in heavy motion. Truth hit Trouble with two bricks, and Andre and Black D with a half a key. Truth hit Boss with six bricks and Mileena with five. He had sixteen and a half bricks left, which he knew would be sold in a week or so. Truth and Jazzie continued to have relationship issues, and she continued to visit Law.

Detective Bryant spent days searching for Jazzie around Milwaukee but couldn't find any leads on her where abouts. He had no idea Jazzie switched up cars, so he was running in circles. Detective Bryant never went in to get questioned about the homicide, so he was on the run and hiding out with a dope fiend he had been tricking with.

Detective Bryant shaved all his hair off and grew a thick beard to conceal his identity. He also stopped bathing so he could disguise himself as a crack head. This wasn't the first time he had to go deep cover on the streets to catch a drug dealer, so being grungy didn't bother him.

"Law, I think Truth know about us," Jazzie confessed.

"So! Fuck that square ass nigga, you my bitch now!" Law snapped.

"I know, but if he finds out I'm visiting you he gone kill me," Jazzie cried.

"Step yo' game up then, bitch. You was my bottom ho, didn't you learn anything while you was ten toes down with a pimp!"

Tears started to form in Jazzie's eyes as she stuttered out her words, "Y –Y- Y -Yes, I- I -I did, but what's taking so l- l- l- long for y- y- your appeal to go through?"

Jazzie wiped away the tears before they started to leak down her face.

"Detective Bryant was supposed to turn himself in, but he never did. My lawyer said he's gone be on the Milwaukee most wanted list soon. Dig this bitch, they found his DNA on the victim's body, which links him to the crime scene. So the judge is gone overturn my case. You got that money yet?"

Jazzie turned her head away from Law then stared down at the floor as she responded, "Nope, Truth is so damn secretive, at the most he'll leave 10G's laying around, and I don't know where the rest of his stash is at."

The look on Law's face was so menacing that Jazzie started to perspire. The disgust he had for Jazzie couldn't be disguised. Law grabbed Jazzie's hand, squeezing it as hard as he could.

The pain was so excruciating Jazzie's face started to turn red as she cried, "Stop Law, you hurting me!"

One of the C.O.'s working in the visiting room noticed some unacceptable contact between Law and Jazzie and grew a bit concerned. The C.O. stood up and walked over towards Law and Jazzie to see if everything was alright.

"I don't mean to be nosey, but is everything okay between you two? I noticed the young lady crying, and we can't allow any disruption taking place on Federal property."

Jazzie quickly gathered herself then replied with a quick lie, "I'm fine, my man just gave me some good news, and I'm emotional right now."

Jazzie gave the C.O. a fake smile to ease the tension in the air.

"Okay, I'm sorry for bothering you two."

"No problem C.O.," Law returned with a wicked grin.

"I don't see why these dumb black bitches drive way up here to see these losers. I bet they treated them like shit when they were out," the C.O. whispered as he strolled back to his post.

"Now, back to what I was saying, you got one week to get my money or that's yo' ass Jazzie."

"O – O- O okay Daddy, I'll get on top of my business, I swear," Jazzie whined.

"I know you will bitch, now give Daddy some suga. You make sure I don't come home broke now."

Jazzie and Law embraced each other one last time before the visit ended. As Jazzie left the prison, she wondered how she was gone snake Truth out of a 100 G'z without losing her life in the process.

****

Over the course of time, Boss became envious of Truth. He loved the fact that he had dirt on Jazzie and that he could use it against her and shit on Truth if he wanted to. Boss stuck his key into the ignition of his Lexus when Jazzie suddenly pulled up.

Boss honked his horn, signaling Jazzie over to his car. Jazzie grabbed her purse then sashayed over towards Boss' whip.

"What's good Boss?" Jazzie uttered as she leaned on Boss' car door, revealing her ass crack and thong to the public.

"Hop in; I need to holla at cha."

Jazzie was oblivious as to why Boss needed to holla at her. She surveyed the area before hopping in the car. The Lexus' soft leather seats gripped Jazzie's butt cheeks as she sunk into the seat. She thought it was strange the way Boss said, 'I need to holla at cha.' That usually meant something bad happened or somebody had some good news in the hood, but you never could tell 'til you chopped it up with that person.

"Jazzie, you know I keeps my eyes and ears to the street at all times, right? A lil birdy told me some disturbing shit that wasn't suppose to made it back to me."

"Really?" Jazzie replied, looking dumbfounded.

"I been wondering if I should keep this info I got on you from my boy or use it to my advantage," Boss declared as he rubbed his chin hairs.

Jazzie suddenly became irritate wondering where Boss was going with his charades.

"And your point is?" Jazzie stated sarcastically.

"Well, I know you been going to visit yo' ex, Law," Boss shot back while sucking on his teeth.

Jazzie's heart felt like it just exploded. She tried to remain calm and keep her composure, but she knew she was in some shit now.

"No I haven't, that nigga old news. Wherever you got yo' info from they spent you, Boss."

"I figured you'd deny it, Jaz. That's why I followed you and videotaped you. You remember the time you lied to Truth 'bout being at Gurnee Mills with Raquel shopping?"

Jazzie had to think for a second, "Yeah, the fuck that got to do with anything?"

"Well, Truth called me that night while me and Raquel were arguing, and he heard her in the background. He told me you said yawl were together, damn you sloppy. Truth wanted me to bring Raquel up to La Joy's to bust you out, but I covered fo' you and told him you probably was shopping fo' his birthday gift and to just chill."

A wicked grin flashed on Boss face. He felt like he was breaking Jazzie down to where he wanted her at. Jazzie felt a bit relieved after listening to Boss, yet wondered why he was protecting her. She reached in her Coach purse then tossed Boss a wad of money.

"Whoa, what you doing, girl? I don't want yo' money. Anyway, this ain't enough money fo' what I did fo' yo' ass no way."

Jazzie knew this would come down to her having to throw Boss some pussy to keep him at bay. Jazzie hoped after she fucked Boss it would be the end of his lil blackmail game. Suddenly Boss pulled off and hit a few corners. Jazzie had no idea where Boss was taking her, she just wanted to hop back in her car and think. Jazzie knew leaving Boss' presence was not an option, so she thought quickly.

"Let's go to one of yo' duck off spots so I can take care of you, Boss." Jazzie whispered softly while rubbing on his inner thigh.

Boss hadn't planned on Jazzie giving in so fast.

"Ok. But you gotta trail me cuz if Raquel see yo' car parked in front of her house knowing I just left, she gone be suspicious."

Boss pulled up beside Jazzie's car and let her out. Jazzie kept wondering how Boss got the ups on her. She didn't like that one bit. Jazzie told herself she wasn't 'bout to be the one that came out on the shitty end of the stick, those days were over with. These young niggaz always thinking with they dicks. Fuck that, I'm gone get his ass before he snitch on me, Jazzie thought.

Jazzie trailed Boss to a house on 34th N Thurston. Boss had it all planned out, he was gone tape them having sex so he could continue blackmailing Jazzie and fucking her whenever he wanted to. Once inside, Boss told Jazzie to wait in the living room because he had to clean up a lil. Jazzie grew suspicious. Her hoe senses kicked in once Boss walked away.

Jazzie peeped Boss' weak game. This nigga in there setting up a camera, so typical of his narrow-minded ass, talkin' 'bout he gotta clean up. He gone be in for a rude awakening when I creep that tape from his ass. Jazzie played along with Boss lil game.

"Can I have something to drink before I fuck yo' brains out?" Jazzie uttered loud enough for Boss to hear.

Boss stepped out of the room once he had the camcorder in the right position.

"What you sipping on, brown or white?"

"Brown will do," Jazzie stated seductively.

Boss reached in his cabinet, grabbed a wine flute then poured Jazzie a double shot of Remy Martin VSOP.

"Fuck it, I'll drink some too," Boss decided as he poured himself a triple shot and sat down next to Jazzie.

Jazzie slammed her drink then gazed at her empty glasses. Instantly she then took off her shirt and tossed it on the floor.

"Damn, itz hot in here nigga, what you ain't got A/C?"

Boss grinned, he purposely turned the A/C off so Jazzie would get hot and start taking off her clothes.

"It is hot in here," Boss agreed as he took off his Polo shirt, revealing his tattoos and chiseled chest.

Jazzie licked her lips as she gently caressed her hard nipples.

"Let me see what you working with, nigga, pull that anaconda out."

Boss slid out of his pants and boxers immediately. Jazzie slowly caressed Boss' dick 'til it was fully erect, then licked around the tip gently sending jolts of electricity through Boss' body.

Jazzie stood up then led Boss back to his room; she decided to turn the game up on him.

"My mouth dry Boss, can you please get me some ice? I got this lil trick I wanna try on you. Truth loves when I do it to him. I'll hold yo' drink for you 'til you come back."

Boss was so horny it never crossed his mind what she could do to his drink while he was gone. Jazzie reached in her purse and retrieved a bottle of Visine. She put five drops inside Boss' drink then stirred it with her finger. Boss came back with a small bucket of ice and his dick in his hand smiling.

"This   enough
ice?" "Yup."

"I know you 'bout to do some shit I never experienced before," Boss stated eagerly.

Jazzie grinned knowing she had the ball in her corner now.

"Drink the rest of yo' drink first, I want you to beat this pussy up."

Jazzie placed a piece of ice inside her warm mouth then inserted his dick in her mouth. The hotness from her mouth mixed with the coldness from the ice sent a tingling sensation through Boss' body. He never had his dick sucked like that.

"Damn, this how you suck Truth dick? Ol' lucky ass nigga."

Boss grabbed a hand full of Jazzie's hair then slowly started stroking her mouth. Boss suddenly became light-headed, so he pulled his dick out of Jazzie's mouth then sat down on his bed. Jazzie grinned. She knew the Visine was kicking in.

"What's wrong?"

"My legs started getting weak, you might as well get on top and ride this big dick. I wanna see if that pussy good as Truth be saying it is," Boss instructed Jazzie as he leaned back on his bed.

Jazzie reached inside her purse and retrieved a Rough Rider condom. She got in the 69 position, peeled the wrapper off the condom and slid it on Boss. So Truth telling this nigga 'bout how my pussy is I swear niggaz ain't shit, Jazzie thought as she stroked Boss' snake.

Jazzie turned around with one of her titties in her mouth as she slid Boss' snake inside her moist womb. She started gyrating slowly savoring the moment, she wanted to bust a nut before Boss passed out, but she knew that wasn't likely.

"Damn this dick good," Jazzie moaned as Boss started to fade out. "Go to sleep nigga, I got something for yo' punk ass," Jazzie muttered to herself.

Boss' body eventually slumped over. Jazzie slapped Boss, making sure he was out. Once he didn't respond, she slowly stepped off of Boss shaking her head while smiling.

"You done fucked up, Boss. You not gone like what I'm 'bout to do to yo' ass."

Jazzie called up her gay cousin Vick and told him to rush over to her asap because she had one to go. Twenty minutes later Vick made it over to Boss' house. Jazzie led him to Boss' room. Vick started licking his lips when he saw who it was Jazzie had for him.

"Gurl, thanks for setting him out, I been wanting to fuck Boss for a long time. I'm gone savor every moment of this."

Jazzie cracked a smile as Vick lubed himself up with some KY jelly.

"Be gentle with him, cuz," Jazzie joked. "Gurl, I'm 'bout to break his ass off."

To be continued

ABOUT THE AUTHOR

Jock Phenix was born in Lake Providence, Louisiana then later moved to Milwaukee, Wisconsin. After reading "The Coldest Winter Ever" By Sistah Souljah he started reading more Urban Street Novels and studying the craft. Jock felt a sense of connection to the stories he read due to the fact that he was living the lifestyle the Street Lit Authors were writing about and decided it was time to pick up the pen and pad and tell his story.

In 2011 Jock Phenix started working on his first novel titled "Frenemiez" based on his life. Currently Jock is a Realtor and Homestead Realty INC, and works closely with banks assessing properties.